Cocktails and Murder

BAREFOOT SLEUTH MYSTERIES

BOOK THREE

H.Y. HANNA

Contents

Chapter One

"You've never had any cocktail other than a piña colada?"

Ellie Bishop smiled sheepishly at the young man who was staring at her, aghast.

"I like piña coladas," she said defensively.

"Yes, but surely you must have tried something else?"

Ellie shook her head. "That's what I always order."

"Well, we've got to do something about that," he declared. "You can't come to Florida and not taste some other cocktails! And you're with the best person to help you do that," he added with a wink. "Ask anyone in the Tampa Bay area and they'll tell you that Rob Saunders is the top local expert on cocktails. My workshop is the perfect introduction to mixology and the best way to sample some of the most popular cocktails out there."

"Yes, it sounded really intriguing when I saw the poster in the resort lobby," said Ellie. "It's why I signed up for it. Besides, who wouldn't want to do a cocktail class in this setting?" she added with a grin and gestured to their surroundings: the enormous swimming pool on one side, surrounded by cabanas and lounge chairs, and the view of the beach on the other. The sky above them was blue and cloudless, and the afternoon sun was warm on their faces.

Rob grinned as well, his teeth looking very white in contrast to his tanned face.

"Yeah, it was awesome of the Sunset Palms Beach Resort to let me hold my workshop at their Tiki Bar. I'm in talks with them to hold a regular event every month."

"Oh, I'm sure lots of guests would love that," said Ellie, glancing at the group of ladies next to her, who were all waiting for the cocktail workshop to start.

"Are we really going to taste every famous cocktail out there?" one of the women spoke up. "Surely we can't go through that many in two hours?"

Rob Saunders laughed. "No, we'll just be doing rum cocktails today, but it's as good a place to start as any, especially when you're vacationing in Florida! Now gather around, ladies, and I'll show you some of the secret weapons of the mixologist."

The other women flocked forward eagerly. Ellie wondered cynically if it was as much to get closer to their host as it was to learn how to mix cocktails. With his boyish good looks, megawatt smile, and smooth manner, Rob Saunders was obviously a hit with the ladies.

What a shame Aunt Olive didn't come to do the workshop with me, thought Ellie with a wry smile. *She would have loved Rob!*

Aunt Olive was her father's much older—and much more eccentric—sister. She was a wealthy widow who lived her life still very much like the carefree hippie she used to be, and Ellie adored her. Having grown up in a family of stuffy, respectable types who were only concerned with having a stable job and a secure future, Ellie was so grateful to have a godmother who understood her longing for excitement and adventure.

In fact, she wouldn't even have been here at this cocktail class, if it weren't for Aunt Olive. Ellie had been stuck in a rut back in London, following a dreary routine of commuting to her boring temp job and trying to adapt to living with her parents again after her boyfriend of three years had cheated on her. With Christmas just around the corner, the holiday period had seemed pretty miserable, with nothing to look forward to except more cold, grey weather... until the letter from Aunt Olive had arrived, with a plane ticket and an invitation to come and join her at a beach resort in Florida!

It hadn't taken Ellie long to decide to swap her cup of afternoon tea for a tropical cocktail. Before she knew it, she was here at the Sunset Palms Beach Resort, with a white sand beach and the sparkling blue waters of the Gulf of Mexico on her doorstep. And since arriving, her life had been a rollercoaster of excitement, not least because she had become inadvertently entangled in two murders!

But that's all behind me, Ellie reminded herself. Now she had weeks of glorious balmy weather ahead of her, with nothing to do except enjoy the resort facilities. *And the only mystery I'm going to tackle is how to shake a good cocktail*, she thought with a smile, turning back to listen to Rob Saunders.

"...no one's quite sure where the name 'cocktail' came from. There are all sorts of stories: like some say it's named after the French word *'coquetier,'* which means 'egg cup,' or that the name came from mixed drinks in Mexico that were stirred with a chicken feather... but the one that I like best is that it comes from the 'cocked tail' of a perky horse. See, horse dealers in the 1700s used to use ginger to make their animals raise their tails and look spirited. So adding spices like ginger or pepper to drinks became known as 'cock-tail.'" Rob grinned. "Kinda neat, huh? Now I'm gonna to show you how to make some of the most famous rum cocktails... starting with the mojito!"

"*MIAOW?*"

Ellie looked down and saw a sleek black cat standing by her ankles. It was the resort cat, who happened to be named "Mojito," and she had obviously thought that she was being called.

"No, we're not talking about you," said Ellie, chuckling and bending down to give the cat a pat.

Mojito evaded her hand and jumped up to sit on a stool beside Ellie, from which she could see over the bar counter. She watched with interest as Rob Saunders added fresh mint leaves, sugar syrup, and lime chunks to a highball glass, and crushed them gently with a muddler. Then he turned to the array of liquor bottles on the shelves behind him and lifted a bottle of Bacardi. Whirling back, he poured a measure of it into a jigger with great flourish, then tipped the rum into the glass, before topping it up with club soda and ice. Ellie found his dramatic manner a bit irritating; it was obvious that the man loved himself and was enjoying the rapt attention of the ladies around him. But she had to admit that Rob Saunders was a pretty good showman.

"Tada!" he said, making a sweeping gesture with one hand toward the finished drink. "Classic, refreshing, and it'll take you to a sun-drenched beach with a single sip. For many people, the mojito is the perfect rum cocktail. Did you know that it was one of Ernest Hemingway's favorite drinks?" He passed out sets of cocktail equipment to the women standing around the bar. "Now it's your turn."

Everyone got to work trying to replicate his creation. Ellie filled the bottom of her glass with the fresh mint leaves, sugar syrup, and lime chunks, and used the muddler to mash them gently together. The action released the aromatic oils in the mint leaves, and they rose up, mingling with the scent of the fresh lime juice.

"Mmm..." said Ellie, leaning forward to press her nose over the opening of the glass and inhaling appreciatively.

"*MIAOW?*" said Mojito, leaning forward and trying to thrust her little nose into the glass as well.

"No, no," laughed Ellie, pulling the glass out of the cat's reach. "Not for you."

She picked up her jigger and bit her bottom lip in concentration as she poured out the required amount of rum into the measuring device. Her hands slipped and a bit of rum dribbled over the edge and into the glass.

"Oh bugger!" Ellie muttered. Now she didn't know how much rum had already gone into the glass.

She looked up, intending to ask Rob Saunders if she should start again, and was surprised to see that he had left his station behind the bar. Glancing around, she saw him several feet away, hurrying after an older man who was walking past the pool deck. Rob put an urgent hand on the older man's arm, stopping him, and as the wind shifted, their voices drifted over to Ellie:

"...gotta speak to you, Uncle Walt."

The older man looked at him impatiently. "What do you want, boy?"

"It's that thing we talked about last week. I sent you the proposal... My new business idea, remember?"

"The cocktail bar?" said the older man scornfully. "That was the dumbest proposal I've ever read. Really lame."

Rob flushed an angry red and glanced around, as if to see if anyone had heard. "It's not lame," he hissed. "It's a great concept and I can prove it, if you'll just help me out with a bit of investment money!"

"What makes you think I would *want* to invest in a start-up?" said his uncle.

"You seem to hand out money to random losers out there," said Rob bitterly. "So why not your own nephew?"

The older man glowered at him. "They're not 'random losers,' but I wouldn't expect *you* to understand. I didn't make my millions from being an idiot. I've yet to make a poor investment decision. Even though I'm usually a silent partner and don't get involved in the day-to-day running of things, I keep my finger on the pulse."

"Look, Uncle Walt, can't you just give me a chance? I know I can make this work! I just need some capital to help me get started."

"Ask the bank, then."

"The bank?" spluttered Rob. "The bank would charge me crazy fees and interest on a loan!"

"So? It's what everyone else has to deal with."

"Yeah, but why should I lose money

to the stupid bank when you can give me the money interest-free? Not that you're really *giving* me the money," Rob hastened to add. "You're *investing* it—and you'll be making it back. I promise you'll double it within a year."

"Making a rash promise like that just shows how little you know about business," said his uncle impatiently. "Anyway, I haven't got time for this now."

"But I can show you—"

"Not now," snapped his uncle. "I've got a meeting in a moment with Roy Mack."

"The alligator farm guy?" said Rob contemptuously. "I can't believe you're turning your nose up at my business proposal but you're happy to invest in that dump!"

"That 'dump' happens to be a successful local tourist attraction and supplier of gator meat and hide," said

Walter Saunders. "Since I invested in it five years ago, it's brought me a tidy sum in profits every year—which is more than I can say I've ever got from you, boy!"

Rob stood fuming and staring after his uncle as the latter stalked off. Then he turned back toward the Tiki Bar and caught Ellie watching him. She flushed and hastily looked away. He sauntered over toward her and said, his smooth smile back in place:

"So, how's it going?"

"Oh… erm… I think I might have mucked up," mumbled Ellie. She held up her jigger and explained about spilling the rum.

"Ah, if it's just a little slip, don't worry about it. Nothing wrong with a little extra kick now and then," said Rob with wink. He stood and watched as she completed the steps in the mojito recipe, then gestured for her to take a sip.

Ellie was surprised by how refreshing the drink was. It wasn't anywhere near as sweet as her beloved piña colada, but she had to admit that it was very nice, especially on a hot day like today. Before she realized it, she had drained half the glass and looked up to see Rob watching her with delight.

"Like it?" he asked.

Ellie nodded. "I still wouldn't order it over a piña colada though," she said, laughing.

Rob, giving her a flirtatious smile. "Guess I'll have to work harder to change your mind then!"

Chapter Two

Over the next two hours, Ellie learned how to make the classic daiquiri, the wonderfully sweet Hurricane, the flamboyant Jungle Bird, and—last but not least—the infamous Tiki cocktail: the Scorpion Bowl. By the time the class was over, she was feeling quite lightheaded from all the alcohol she had sampled! She stumbled slightly as she left the Tiki Bar and crossed the pool deck, and heard a familiar male voice say behind her:

"Whoa... looks like you've been enjoying yourself at the cocktail class!"

Ellie turned to see a black man smiling at her and recognized one of her favorite people at the resort: Sol, the head waiter at the *Hammerheads Bar and Grill*. Calm and kind, with a warm charisma and a ready smile for everyone, Sol had become a firm friend and even a bit of a fatherly presence. He always seemed to keep an eye out for Ellie and make sure that she was all right. Now he gave her a look of mock reproach.

"You been keeping hydrated? It's really important to drink lots of water to dilute the alcohol," he said. "Hang on— stay there. I'll be back in a minute."

He returned a few moments later with a tall glass of cold water. "Here... drink it all up."

Ellie took the glass and gulped it down gratefully.

"Like I always tell my daughter, if you're gonna drink, make sure you down a glass of water for every glass of booze," said Sol, adding with a sigh: "Not that she should be drinking at all, being underage and all, but you know, you can't always stop them doing stuff, so I figure it's better to teach 'em how to look after themselves."

"You have a daughter?" asked Ellie with a smile. She could just imagine what a great father Sol must be—the kind of father she wished she had. Not that she didn't love her own dad, of course, but Mr. Bishop was staid and stuffy, always worrying about her job prospects or her finances, and always disapproving of her life choices. *I'll bet Sol is a lot more tolerant and understanding as a father*, Ellie thought. He already seemed to take a practical approach to his daughter's rebelliousness.

"Yup, my Jasmine has just turned eighteen." Sol laughed and shook his head. "Can't believe it sometimes. My little girl is all grown up! There were times when I thought I'd never be able to do it on my own." He paused and, seeing Ellie's inquiring look, he added, "My wife died when Jasmine was still little, you see."

"Oh, I'm sorry," said Ellie. "I didn't realize that you're a single dad. Wow, that must be really tough."

"It hasn't always been easy," Sol admitted. "A girl really needs a woman's touch, you know? It's hard for a father to understand what's going on inside her head sometimes. But Jasmine's a good girl; I know she is. Even if she does get herself into trouble sometimes..." A shadow crossed his face, then he brightened. "Anyway, I hope you'll get the chance to meet her someday."

"I'd love that," said Ellie. "Does she ever come to the resort?"

"Sometimes. She's got a part-time job over at the marina, opposite the beach, you know? So it's not that far. Sometimes she comes over to see her old man after her shift and we ride home together." He nodded at the empty glass. "You want another? Or how about you come over to *Hammerheads* and I serve you up a nice, cool glass of our famous Florida orange juice?"

"That sounds wonderful—just what I need," said Ellie, following him as he headed toward the restaurant.

"So where's your aunt this afternoon? She didn't do the cocktail class with you?"

"No, she's having a massage over at the spa," Ellie explained. She glanced sideways at Sol, noticing for the first time that he wasn't wearing his usual uniform of polo shirt and khakis. Instead, he was wearing a camp shirt with a vibrant tropical palm print over smart chino shorts.

"Hey... have you got a new uniform?"

she asked.

Sol looked pleased that she'd noticed. "Yup. The resort is thinking of upgrading our look and I've been given a trial set to do a test run—you know, make sure it's comfortable and allows easy movement, before they commission a full batch." He pointed to the apron around his waist. "What do you think of the logo? Nice touch, huh?"

Ellie bent closer to look and saw that the apron had a large logo embroidered in the corner, showing a hammerhead shark swimming between the words "Bar" and "Grill."

"Oh, I love it!" she said. "Are all the restaurants at the resort going to have personalized staff aprons, each with their own logos?"

"That's the idea. But we're the first," said Sol with a smug smile. "And I have to say, so far, this new uniform gets a major thumbs-up from me! It's so much cooler and easier to move in."

They mounted the steps to the outdoor terrace of the restaurant and walked across to the main entrance.

"So are you and your aunt coming over to *Hammerheads* for dinner this evening?" asked Sol. "We've got a new special: honey-glazed Chilean sea bass with pineapple relish and jewel potatoes—and for dessert: red velvet fudge cake with white-chocolate-Amaretto frosting."

"Mmm, that sounds delicious! But actually... erm... I've got a date," said Ellie, blushing slightly.

Sol raised his eyebrows and gave her a teasing smile. "Anyone I know?"

Before she could reply, they bumped into a group of people just inside the door of the restaurant: a young mother leading a little boy with a bleeding nose, who was crying loudly, and a handsome young man with sun-streaked brown hair who was talking gently to the child. Ellie's heart skipped a beat as the young man looked up and their eyes met. Well, it would have been hard for any woman not to feel her pulse quicken when she looked at Dr. Blake Thornton. With his tall, athletic figure and laughing brown eyes, he was the kind of man who turned female heads wherever he went.

And I've got a date with him tonight, Ellie thought with an inward smile. Then she felt a familiar twinge of unease. This was their third date now and she still wasn't sure she was doing the right thing. She had been determined to avoid any romantic entanglements during her time in Florida. After all, she was only here on vacation for a few weeks and she would be returning home to England in the new year.

But somehow, life had a way of sabotaging her best-laid plans. There had been instant chemistry between them when she'd met Blake, and it had been hard for her to resist the charming resort doctor, especially when he'd made it so obvious that he wanted to get to know her better. Still, she had deliberately kept things light and casual between them. Even though they'd been on two dates already, they still hadn't even shared a proper kiss yet.

I'm just enjoying it as a fun flirtation, Ellie reminded herself. She wasn't going to fall in love or do anything silly like that. Having just come out of a three-year relationship which had ended disastrously, the last thing she needed right now was to get involved again— especially with someone on the other side of the Atlantic!

Still, watching Blake now and seeing the calm and gentle way he soothed the frightened child, Ellie couldn't help feeling a rush of admiration. Blake produced a lollipop from his pocket and distracted the little boy while he pinched the boy's nose and applied pressure until the bleeding stopped.

"Oh, thank you so much, doc," said the boy's mother gratefully as she watched her son happily suck on the lollipop, his tears forgotten. "I've told Ethan so many times not to pick his nose, but he just won't listen!"

Blake chuckled. "It's the age," he assured her. "I'm sure he'll grow out of it. Don't worry, after today's episode, Ethan will probably think twice before sticking his finger up his nostrils in the future!"

Sol helped the young mother and her little boy back to their table while Blake turned to Ellie with a big smile.

"I'm really looking forward to tonight," he said. "You still okay to meet at seven o'clock in the lobby?"

Ellie nodded. "Do I need to get dressed up or anything?"

"Oh no, we're not going anywhere fancy. It's a local fish shack I've been wanting to show you. They do amazing grouper sandwiches there. Anyway, you always look great," he added, his eyes glowing appreciatively.

Ellie was annoyed to find herself blushing. *Stop behaving like a silly, lovestruck schoolgirl!* she admonished herself. Trying to act cool, she smiled and said, "Thanks. Well, I'll see you later then."

After Blake left, Ellie decided to sit outside and chose the table in the far corner of the terrace. It was her favorite table at the restaurant. A huge potted palm next to the table obscured her from the view of the other diners, and her seat at the edge of the terrace gave her a vista across the pool deck and out toward the beach in the distance. The combo meant that she could sit and people-watch in total privacy, something Ellie loved doing. The Sunset Palms Beach Resort attracted all sorts of guests and visitors, and Ellie never tired of observing people and speculating about their backgrounds.

She noticed a fascinating man coming down the walkway from the main resort building. He looked almost like an American "Crocodile Dundee" with his wide-brimmed hat jammed low over his head and a necklace of white triangular teeth around his neck. His face was tanned and leathery, and he wore a long-sleeved camouflage print shirt paired with khaki shorts and tough leather boots. He looked so outlandish that Ellie wondered if he was part of a crew shooting a movie or TV show at the resort. Then she saw him stride toward *Hammerheads* and, a minute later, he entered the restaurant.

The man came out onto the terrace and paused for a moment, scanning the tables. Then to Ellie's surprise, he came directly toward her.

Chapter Three

Ellie was just wondering what the strange man wanted when she realized that he was actually heading for a table next to hers. It was on the other side of the giant potted palm and she hadn't paid any attention when she sat down, but now she realized that there was a man sitting there. In fact, it was someone she recognized: the older man that Rob Saunders had been talking to— his uncle, Walter Saunders. And remembering their conversation, Ellie guessed that the newcomer was the alligator farm owner, Roy Mack. Hidden by the bushy fronds of the potted palm between them, she watched their meeting with avid curiosity.

"Hey Walt! Good to see you, man!"

Walter Saunders looked up at the other man but didn't return his smile. "Hello Roy," he said. "You're late."

"Sorry, I only got your call last night and I had some other things planned today. Had to reshuffle my plans real quick. Hey, you never told me that you were coming to Florida," Roy Mack complained. "If I knew you were coming, I coulda given you a better welcome! Some great new bars opened up and we could do a tour of the—"

"This isn't a vacation trip, Roy," growled Saunders. "I'm here to talk business."

"Well, sure, man! But we can still have a drink while we're talking, right?" Mack beckoned to one of the waitresses who had been hovering nearby.

"Yes, sir?" she said. She was a pretty

girl of about eighteen and she was eyeing them in a way that suggested she was wondering if they would leave her a big tip.

"What'll you have, Walt? It's on me," said Mack.

"I'll have a whiskey, on the rocks."

"Aww, come on, man! You're not gonna order a boring old whiskey, are you? You're at a beach resort, for Pete's sake! Have a cocktail. I hear they do great tiki cocktails at this place." Roy Mack leaned toward the older man and said in a mock whisper: "Can you take the strong stuff?"

"Of course." Saunders looked amused. "Most tiki cocktails are just like fruit punches anyway."

"Hey man! That's not true," cried Mack indignantly. "Some of them can pack a real wallop. I once went on a tiki bender and I swear, I woke up on Monday not remembering a single thing

I did that whole weekend."

"So, what do you want me to do: order a Jungle Juice or a Zombie?" said Saunders with amused contempt.

"I guess everyone always talks about those, but I was thinking of the Scorpion Bowl actually."

"The Scorpion Bowl?" Saunders gave an incredulous laugh. "Are you kidding me? That's a punch bowl for college kids to share. That's no challenge at all."

"Not if you drink the whole bowl by yourself," said Mack smugly.

Saunders pulled a face. "I'm not drinking a whole bowl of punch."

"Have you actually tasted it?" challenged Mack.

"No, but I don't need to. I've seen what it looks like." Saunders pulled a disgusted face. "Stupid ceramic bowl with hula girls and all that fruit floating in the bowl. It's even got flowers on top!"

"It's also got rum, gin, and brandy," said Mack. "And it's ranked as one of the strongest tiki cocktails out there."

"Oh, all right," said Saunders, sitting back in his chair. "Order me one! We'll see if I can't drink a bowl of your stupid punch."

When the two Scorpion Bowls arrived, however, and Saunders tasted his drink, Ellie saw an expression of reluctant appreciation cross his face.

"Whaddya think, man… not bad, eh?" said Roy Mack, grinning and elbowing the older man.

"It's better than I expected," Saunders admitted, ignoring the straw and drinking directly from the bowl.

"There, you see? I told you so," said Mack, gloating. Then he held up a hand eagerly. "Wait, wait… I gotta add something…"

He reached into his shirt pocket and pulled out a small leather pouch—the kind often used for keeping jewelry. But when he opened it and shook its contents onto his palm, Ellie saw that it actually contained several small brown items. They looked like shriveled bugs. She leaned forward to peer through a gap in the palm tree for a better look, then recoiled as she realized what they were: dried scorpions.

"What are those?" asked Saunders, eying them warily.

"Manchurian scorpions," said Mack with glee. He held his palm out to the other man. "Go on—pick one up," he taunted.

Saunders hesitated, then gingerly picked one shriveled specimen from the pile on Mack's hand and brought it closer to his face to examine it.

"Comes from China. Totally dehydrated and 100% edible. Pretty awesome, huh?" said Mack. "It's a new product we're selling in the gator farm gift shop. Really popular with the tourists. You can eat the pinchers, tail, stinger—everything!"

Before the other man could stop him, he reached across and plucked the dried scorpion out of Saunders's hand, then dropped it into his cocktail. Then Mack fished another scorpion out of the pile and dropped it into his own drink as well.

"Now they really are 'Scorpion Bowls'!" he said with satisfaction.

"What did you do that for?" Saunders complained. "I don't want a stupid bug in my drink!"

"Hey, they're not bugs, man—they're arachnids," said Mack. "And they're really good for you, you know. Like, full of vitamins and minerals and stuff. The Chinese have eaten them for thousands of years. They've got great medicinal benefits like boosting the blood system and making you stronger. They even say—" He leaned closer to the older man and elbowed him, his grin becoming lascivious. "—that they're better than Viagra. Know what I mean?" He waggled his eyebrows. "Hey, a man in your position, with a hot young wife… you'll want all the help you can get, huh? What's the age difference between you and the new Mrs. Saunders? Like, thirty years?"

"None of your business," snapped Saunders.

Using his straw, he stirred his drink in disgust until he finally fished out the dried scorpion. Dumping it on the table beside the cocktail, he wiped his hands, then turned back to Roy Mack. "Enough with your crap, Roy. I'm here on serious business."

"OK, OK, I'm just having a bit of fun," said Roy Mack sulkily. He picked up his Scorpion Bowl and took several swallows before smacking his lips loudly and sitting back. "So... what d'you wanna talk about?"

"The company accounts," said Saunders. "My accountant has been going over the records and he says there's a discrepancy."

"What discrepancy?" said Mack, looking bewildered. "I sent you all the books, just like you asked for!"

"Yes, but the numbers don't add up," said Saunders. "I don't know whether due to your stupidity in bookkeeping or deliberate deception—"

"What? Are you accusing me of cheating you?" demanded Mack.

"I'm not accusing you of anything... yet," said Saunders. "I'm saying I want to do a further audit."

"You wanna come and check up on me? What are you... like, my math teacher?" said Mack angrily. "That's not cool, man! I don't know how you guys do things up north, but down here in

Florida, we trust each other."

"This isn't about trust. This is about protecting my investment," said Saunders shortly. "I want to personally check what you're doing at the farm—"

"You *know* what we're doing!" said Mack with a laugh. "We're breeding gators. We're selling their meat and their hides. We're showing 'em to tourists... Jeez, man, what do you think we're doing?" He thumped a hand on the table. "OK, fine. You wanna come check? Be my guest. Come over to the farm tomorrow and I'll personally show you around. I'll take you behind every closed door, open every damned drawer and cupboard in that place, give you access to every file we've got. You can look all you like. Knock yourself out. I guarantee you won't find anything."

"We'll see," said Saunders grimly. "I'll be over at the farm at ten o'clock sharp."

"Looking forward to it," said Roy

Mack, making a joking salute. He tossed back the rest of his cocktail, then stood up. "Well, I gotta go. See you tomorrow, Walt."

Chapter Four

As Roy Mack was leaving the restaurant, he passed a woman in her thirties just arriving and did an almost comical double-take. In fact, Ellie could see that practically every male guest in the restaurant was gawking at the new arrival. Although the woman wasn't especially beautiful, she had a sort of superficial prettiness which was enhanced by glamorous hair, professional make-up, and extensive plastic surgery. She was also wearing a skimpy bikini with nothing covering it except a sarong tied carelessly around her hips, and it did little to hide her ample assets. From the way she was swaying her hips and tossing her hair over her shoulders, she obviously knew every man's eyes were on her, and she was enjoying the attention.

She sashayed across the terrace and made for Walter Saunders's table, bending to give him a peck on the cheek before sliding into the seat next to him.

"Hi honey—did you miss me?" she asked coquettishly. She looked at the cocktail in front of him. "Omigod, is that a Scorpion Bowl? I can't believe you'd be drinking that! I thought you said tiki cocktails were just for tourists?"

Saunders gave a wry smile. "Yeah, well, this was foisted on me, but I have to admit, I kind of like it." He raised the bowl and took a big gulp, then eyed her indulgently. "What have you been doing, Tonya? I thought you'd be by the pool, but I didn't see you when I walked past earlier."

The woman fluffed her hair. "Oh… I got bored so I went for a walk. The resort has a little shopping mall, you know. Kinda cute. Designer boutiques and an art gallery and chocolate shop… Oh, and you know what, honey? I saw the most divine pair of pearl earrings in the jeweler's window." She leaned toward him. "Can I have them? Please?"

"How many pairs of pearl earrings does a woman need?" grumbled Saunders. "I got you a new pair last week."

"But these are totally different! Those were regular white pearls. These are black pearls, in a platinum and diamond setting. Oh Walt, they're just totally gorgeous!"

"All right, all right," said Saunders good-naturedly. "I'll get them for you tomorrow."

"Thank you!" Tonya threw her arms around his neck and gave him a loud smack on the lips.

Walter Saunders smiled complacently, obviously enjoying the fact that every man in the restaurant was probably envying him. He indicated his cocktail. "So... you want a drink?"

Tonya's lips curled in a malicious smile. "Yeah, but let me order it." She turned and beckoned to the waitress, the same young girl who had served the two men earlier.

"Yes, ma'am?" the girl asked.

"Bring me a Diet Coke."

The waitress disappeared and returned a few minutes later with tray on which stood a tall glass filled with ice and a can of Diet Coke. She was about to place them on a table when Tonya stopped her.

"What's that?" she demanded.

"It's your Diet Coke, ma'am," said the waitress.

"I didn't order Diet Coke!" said Tonya.

The waitress stared at her. "But you did. You said—"

"I said I wanted a Sprite." Tonya waved a hand at the can. "Take this away and bring me what I ordered."

"I'm sorry, ma'am, I thought you said… I'm sorry for the mistake," mumbled the waitress. She left the glass but picked up the can of Diet Coke and returned to the kitchen. A few minutes later, she was back, this time with a can of Sprite, which she set tentatively down on the table.

Tonya glanced at the green can. "Can't you get a simple order right?" she asked "I said I wanted a Fanta."

"No, you… you definitely said Sprite," protested the waitress.

Tonya narrowed her eyes. "Are you calling me a liar?"

"No! But I heard you! You said… you

told me you wanted a Sprite."

"I never said that. I asked for a Fanta." Tonya rolled her eyes and exhaled in an exaggerated manner. "Are you, like, stupid or something? How hard can it be to bring a soft drink?"

The waitress pressed her lips tightly together. She snatched the can of Sprite off the table and stalked back to the kitchen. As soon as she was out of sight, Tonya giggled, looking pleased with herself.

"Tonya..." said Saunders, shaking his head.

"What?" she said, giggling even more. "I'm just having some fun."

Ellie couldn't believe she had heard right. She had been sitting and watching with growing disbelief at the whole scene unfolding next to her. She had never seen anyone behave so outrageously. In fact, she had been so dumbfounded that she hadn't thought to get up and reveal herself, and back up the poor waitress. Now, as she watched the girl returning with yet another soft drink, she vowed to speak up if Tonya continued playing her cruel prank.

The waitress set a can of Fanta down on the table with a thud and stood back, crossing her arms. Tonya looked at the can and let out an outraged gasp. "What's that?"

"It's the Fanta you ordered," said the waitress through clenched teeth.

"I never ordered Fanta," said Tonya. "I said I wanted a cream soda."

"NO, YOU DIDN'T!" yelled the waitress suddenly. She leaned forward, her hands balled into fist. "I know what you're doing! You think it's fun to pick on people like me, huh? Just because you're rich, right? Well, let me tell you something: you're no better than I am and you have no right to treat people like this! Did you think it was funny to—

"

"Enough," growled Walter Saunders. "I don't like your tone of voice, young woman. You have no right to speak to a customer like that."

"I... she was the one who..." spluttered the waitress, seething with fury.

This is ridiculous! thought Ellie. *I've got to say something.* But before she could stand up, Sol arrived on the scene.

"Is there a problem, sir?" he asked politely, eyeing the waitress's red face.

"Yes, there is a damned problem," snapped Saunders. He pointed at the waitress. "Her! She's a rude little brat!"

The waitress started to say something, but Sol put a gentle hand on her arm, then he turned to Walter Saunders and said in a neutral tone: "I'm sorry, sir, about any distress you may have experienced. I don't know what happened here exactly, but I do know my staff. Ava prides herself in her work and would have done her best to serve you. Maybe there's been a misunderstanding?"

"Hell, there was no misunderstanding! All my wife did was ask for a soft drink. Your waitress couldn't even get the order right, then she had the audacity to lecture us—"

"That's not true!" cried the waitress, angry tears springing to her eyes. She pointed at Tonya. "*She* was the one who was playing a prank on me. She kept changing her order and pretending she didn't order stuff—"

"Yes, that's right," said Ellie, suddenly standing up and stepping out from behind the potted palm.

Both Walter Saunders and his wife jerked their heads around in surprise. They obviously hadn't realized that there was another table behind the potted palm and that someone had been sitting there and observing the whole incident.

"I heard everything," said Ellie. "This lady here—" She pointed at Tonya. "—kept changing her order on purpose. She was laughing about it behind Ava's back. It was a stupid, childish prank, but she obviously thought it was funny."

Tonya glared at Ellie. "How dare you—!"

"Who the hell are you?" demanded Saunders, standing up aggressively.

Ellie drew back and Sol hastily stepped forward.

"OK, OK… let's just all calm down…" he said, leaning his hands on the table. Sol was a big man—over six feet tall—and he radiated a calm authority that was hard to ignore. "Please, everybody… sit down again."

Walter Saunders looked like he was going to argue, then he made a noise of disgust and sat down again. Tonya tossed her hair and looked away. Ellie hesitated, then sat down again at her own table. She was itching to really give Tonya a piece of her mind, but she didn't want to make things more difficult for Sol and Ava.

"As I said, I'm sorry again for any confusion and inconvenience," said Sol, his trademark smile firmly in place. "All of us here at *Hammerheads Bar and Grill* are committed to providing the best service possible." He turned to Tonya. "And I will take personal responsibility for your order. Would you mind giving it to me again?"

Tonya gave an exaggerated sigh and said: "Fine! I said I wanted a cream soda. I hope you can get it right *this* time."

Ignoring her provocative words, Sol gave a polite nod and turned toward the kitchen, hustling Ava away with him. A few minutes later, he came back and Ellie had to stifle a chuckle of admiration. Sol was carrying a large tray on which was arranged every single soft drink offered on the restaurant menu. He leaned down and presented the rows and rows of cans and bottles to Tonya Saunders.

"Here you go—you can pick the one you want, just in case there's been any confusion or change of mind."

Tonya flushed angrily, annoyed to find herself thwarted. She reached out with bad grace and plucked a can of cream soda from the lineup. As Sol turned away from the table, Ellie saw Tonya eyeing him with a glint in her eye. It made her uneasy. The look reminded her of a spoiled brat who was resentful at being shown up and was busily plotting revenge.

"Oh, and I want a glass of tomato juice too," Tonya called after Sol's retreating back.

Sol stopped and glanced at her. "Certainly, ma'am. I'll be right back."

He returned a few minutes later

bearing a tall glass of tomato juice. Just as he approached the Saunderses' table, however, Tonya twisted in her seat and, at the same time, Sol tripped and stumbled. He clutched wildly at the glass of tomato juice and luckily caught it before it fell off his tray, but he wasn't able to prevent the red juice sloshing out of the glass. It splashed onto the table and all over the front of Walter Saunders's shirt.

"Hey! What the—!" yelled the businessman, jumping up angrily.

Sol stared in horror. "Oh God—I'm so sorry, sir," he cried. "I don't know what happened... I will make sure you're not charged for anything you order today and I will personally pay for the dry cleaning of your clothes—"

"You bet you will," said Saunders, scowling at him. "You did that on purpose, didn't you?"

"No!" cried Sol. "It was an accident!

Something caught my ankle and—" He broke off as he looked down and realized what must have happened. But he couldn't accuse Tonya of deliberately tripping him without looking like he was being petty.

Ellie saw Tonya lean back, a smile playing at the corners of her lips, and she felt a surge of anger at the other woman's vindictive enjoyment of the situation.

"Ahh—I'm sick and tired of this!" Saunders thundered, standing up. "I pay good money for the top room at this resort and I expect to be treated like a VIP. I won't put up with it—d'you hear me?" He wagged a finger in Sol's face. "I know the owner of this resort and I'm gonna speak to him. Don't think I can't get you fired!"

Chapter Five

There was a tense silence after Walter Saunders stormed out of the restaurant. Tonya got up slowly and, pausing only to shoot Ellie a triumphant look, she started to leave as well. But just as she was about to step away from the table, her cellphone rang. It was a loud, irritating jingle which grated on Ellie's nerves.

"Hiya! What, honey?" Tonya paused, then looked back at the table. "Yeah, it's still there. OK, I'll bring it up." She reached over and scooped up the Scorpion Bowl, then without another word to Sol or Ellie, she sashayed out of the restaurant.

As soon as she was out of earshot, Ellie went up to Sol.

"Oh Sol—I'm so sorry! That woman was vile! It wasn't your fault at all. I saw the whole thing: she tripped you on purpose because she didn't like the way you thwarted her little game. What a vindictive cow! I'm happy to speak to Mr. Papadopoulos and tell him what really happened—"

Sol held a hand up. "That's OK, Ellie. It's real sweet of you and I appreciate it, but I know Mr. Papadopoulos is a fair man and he'll always hear my side of things first. If it was any other place, I'd be worried, but that's one of the best things about working at the Sunset Palms: its owner is a really decent man and the staff here get treated very well."

"Oh. That's good to hear," said Ellie fervently. "I just didn't want you to be punished for their outrageous behavior."

"Don't worry—I've dealt with customers like this before. It's one of the downsides of working at a luxury resort, I guess. You get certain types who think they can get away with anything just because they can leave a big tip." He shrugged. "Most of the time, they're just blowing hot air to make themselves feel more important."

"Well, if you do need me for anything—don't hesitate," insisted Ellie.

Sol gave her a grateful smile. "Thank you. Now, what can I get you? I'm sorry, I got so busy with a customer over on the other side of the restaurant that I totally forgot to bring you a drink! You still want that orange juice?"

"Thanks, but…" Ellie glanced at her watch and gasped. "Yikes! Actually, I've got to go." She grinned at him. "I've got to get ready for my date!"

Ten minutes later, Ellie burst into the

villa suite that she shared with her aunt. She couldn't wait to tell Aunt Olive what had happened at *Hammerheads*. Like all writers, Aunt Olive loved observing others and drew inspiration from real life experiences. She would have been fascinated by the little drama that had played out in the restaurant. Ellie heard the sound of water gushing and found her aunt sitting in the midst of a whirling Jacuzzi bath in her en suite bathroom.

"My goodness, poppet, what an exciting afternoon you've had," said Aunt Olive when Ellie had recounted everything to her. "First the cocktail class, then the eavesdropping—"

"I didn't eavesdrop!" said Ellie indignantly. Then she grinned and said, "Well, OK, maybe a little. It just so happened that the wind was blowing in my direction when Rob Saunders was talking to his uncle, and as for the restaurant, I couldn't help it if I happened to be at the table next to

Walter Saunders."

"Mm… yes, I wish I'd been there to see the whole thing. Not that it was nice for Sol, of course," Aunt Olive added quickly. Then she added with a mischievous smile, "It's a shame this isn't one of my novels, otherwise I could have Tonya Saunders murdered!"

"Aunt Olive!" said Ellie, half-shocked and half-delighted.

"There'd be plenty of suspects too," Aunt Olive continued, leaning back against the side of her tub and narrowing her eyes in thought. "Hmm… yes… the waitress could want revenge and Tonya's lover could have a motive—"

"What lover?" asked Ellie, confused.

Aunt Olive waved a hand. "There's always a lover, especially in a situation like this where a pretty young gold-digger marries a much older man. Of course, Saunders himself could have a motive too, just to make things more complicated. Maybe he wants to get rid of her so he could marry again... Oh, and of course, there's Sol—"

"Not Sol! He could never be a murderer!" cried Ellie. "Sol is the nicest, loveliest man!"

"Calm down, poppet. It's just in a book," said Aunt Olive. "In any case, you don't know what anyone might do when pushed."

"You don't really believe that!" said Ellie. "I mean, do you think that *I* could murder someone in the right circumstances?"

"You might. Who knows? That's the whole point, isn't it? People can act out of character when they're desperate and under pressure."

"I suppose so, but—" Ellie broke off as she caught sight of Aunt Olive's watch on the bathroom vanity. "Oh my God, is that the time? I'm supposed to be getting ready for my date!" she squealed as she whirled and rushed out of her aunt's bathroom.

Ellie raced through her shower and then applied her make-up as quickly as she could, before going to rummage through her wardrobe. Although Blake had said that he wasn't taking her any place fancy, she still wanted to look as nice as possible. Aunt Olive had generously treated her to a couple of new dresses from one of the resort boutiques and now she pulled one of them out. It was a beautiful, off-the-shoulder silk dress in a vivid aquamarine color that brought out the warmth of her skin and enhanced the slight tan that she was beginning to develop.

Ellie held it up against herself and looked critically at her reflection in the mirror. The dress was undeniably gorgeous, but was it too glamorous for a "fish shack"? She didn't want to look overdressed or like she was trying too hard either. Sighing, she returned it to her wardrobe and pulled out the second new dress that her aunt had bought for her. It was a pretty cotton sundress in a deep, rich yellow. She held it up again. Hmm... yes, it wasn't as glamorous as the other dress, but it was probably more suitable.

Ellie shimmied into the dress, then hurriedly brushed her mop of unruly brown curls. With a final dab of lip gloss, she was done. Smiling at her reflection, Ellie grabbed her purse and headed out of the villa, calling goodbye to her aunt as she went. She had barely started down the walkway toward the main resort building, however, when her cellphone rang. She glanced at the screen and saw that it was Blake.

"Hi! Sorry if I'm late! I'm on the way now," she said breathlessly. "I should be in the lobby in a couple of minutes—"

"No, no, that's OK." Blake's voice sounded slightly strange. "Uh... listen,

Ellie… I… uh… D'you mind if we take a raincheck on tonight?" he said in a rush.

Ellie's steps slowed. "A raincheck?" she said. "You mean… you want to cancel?"

"I'm really sorry. Something's come up."

"Oh. Erm… sure. Has a guest got sick?"

"No, it's not that. I…" Blake hesitated. "I'm really sorry, Ellie. You know I wouldn't do this if I could help it."

"Blake, is something wrong?" asked Ellie. "Are you OK? You sound a bit—"

"No, no, everything's fine with me. I'm good," said Blake. "There's just… something I need to do and… and I don't want to keep you waiting—"

"Oh, well, I could come with you if you like," offered Ellie. "I'm not that hungry yet so I don't mind waiting—"

"No!"

Ellie was taken aback by the sharpness in Blake's voice. He must have realized, because his voice softened as he added hastily, "No, it's best if you don't get involved. Look, I'll give you a call tomorrow, OK?"

Before she could answer, Blake hung up. Ellie lowered the phone and stood staring down at it. *What was that all about?* Blake had sounded strange—she was sure she had heard a note of tension in his voice. And had she imagined it or had he seemed secretive about the reason he had to cancel their date suddenly?

With a sigh, she put the phone away, then realized that, while talking to Blake, she had been mindlessly walking and had wandered away from the path to the main resort building. Instead, she had somehow circled around the main pool, and was now on the opposite side of the pool deck from her aunt's villa. The sun had gone down and the area seemed deserted, all the lounge chairs and cabanas already cleaned and tidied, re-arranged back into neat rows.

In front of her, the swimming pool stretched away: an expanse of shimmering blue water, lit by underwater lights. It was empty too, except for a couple in one corner, their arms around each other's necks as they bobbed in the water together. Ellie heard water splashing, and their whispering and laughter drifted over to her. It was a romantic scene and she felt suddenly like she was intruding. She turned away, deciding to take a different route back to her aunt's villa instead of crossing the pool deck and passing the canoodling couple.

The path led away from the deck and circled around a low building on the other side of the pool. It was obviously one of the more exclusive accommodation wings at the resort and faced the beach, like the Beach Villas

Wing, where Aunt Olive's suite was. Rather than being at ground level, though, it seemed to be perched on a slight slope, so that each of the apartment suites inside were elevated. Each had a large balcony that looked out on a spectacular view of the beach.

Ellie paused in front of the building for a moment and saw a sign labelling it as the "Ocean View Wing." She wondered what the suites looked like inside and how they compared to Aunt Olive's suite. She was just about to start walking again when the sound of a cellphone ringing loudly made her jump. She whirled, looking around in confusion, especially as the sound seemed to be coming from *above* her head. Ellie looked up in puzzlement. There were tall palm trees growing next to the building, some of them leaning close to the balconies. But surely someone couldn't be sitting up there in a palm tree, talking on their cellphone?

Then Ellie caught sight of something and laughed. No, maybe not some*one*, but some *parrot,* yes. She looked with affection and exasperation at the huge scarlet macaw perched on one of the palm fronds. Hemingway the resort parrot was up to his old tricks—this time mimicking the mechanical sound of a cellphone ring with amazing accuracy.

"Hi Hemingway!" Ellie called. "What are you doing up there?"

"PEEKABOO!" replied the parrot. "WHATCHA DOIN'?"

Ellie laughed. She knew that Hemingway was just repeating phrases that guests had taught him, but sometimes it was hard not to feel like he really was talking to her. It was amusing but embarrassing as well when she heard the imitation of her own voice, especially when she realized that Hemingway often picked up things she said when she was frustrated and using "strong language"!

"OY! YOU PLONKER! DON'T BE SUCH A KNOB-HEAD!" he said now, tilting his head to look down at her

"Hush, Hemingway!" cried Ellie, trying to contain her horrified laughter. "Don't say things like that! Why can't you learn a nice British phrase? Say… say 'I beg your pardon.'"

The parrot looked down at her.

"Go on, Hemingway—say: 'I beg your pardon.'"

"I BEG YOU."

"No, not: 'I beg you'… 'I beg your pardon.'"

"I BEG YOU."

"Argh!" Ellie rolled her eyes and gave up. "Never mind! I'm going now, Hemingway. You be a good boy. Good night!"

"DON'T LET THE BED BUGS BITE!"

Ellie chuckled as she walked away. She could still hear Hemingway behind her, singing that irritating cellphone ringtone again. *The poor people staying in these suites*, she thought, shaking her head as she rounded the corner of the Ocean View Wing and began taking the path that would circle back toward the main resort building. *I hope Hemingway's not going to remain here singing all night—*

Someone burst out of the side door of the wing and hurtled down the steps, crashing into Ellie with such force that the two of them tumbled to the ground.

"Oomph!" Ellie gasped. She lay stunned for a moment, then slowly rolled over and sat up. She found herself looking at a young woman who was also picking herself up off the ground. She was surprised to see that it was the waitress from *Hammerheads Bar and Grill*.

"Ava?" she said.

The girl had been looking around in a

daze but, at the sound of her name, she jerked around.

"Oh!" she cried. Her eyes were slightly wild and she was breathing quickly.

"Ava, are you OK?" asked Ellie.

The girl blinked. "Yes... I mean, no... there's... there's..." She pointed shakily back at the building.

"What? What is it?" asked Ellie, really starting to feel concerned now. "What's happened?"

Ava pointed mutely at the building again and seemed to be struggling to speak.

"I'll go and look first," said Ellie, patting the girl's arm. "You come after me, OK?"

She mounted the steps to the side door and opened it, finding herself in a long corridor. A series of doors opened off on one side, each one obviously leading into an apartment suite. The first door was open and, when she peered inside, Ellie saw that it led into a spacious living area with a similar design to her aunt's villa. There was a kitchenette on one side and a small dining table on the other, and a large sofa suite next to the floor-to-ceiling French doors, which opened out onto a long balcony with a view of the beach. Everything looked normal.

Taking a deep breath, Ellie stepped inside. She walked slowly into the living room, then froze as she saw what the back of the sofa suite had hidden from view: the body of a man slumped on the floor. It was Walter Saunders.

Ellie hesitated, then hurried over and knelt down next to him. He looked limp and lifeless. Her mind was telling her there was no point but still, she reached out and pressed two fingers against the base of his throat, feeling for a pulse. There was nothing. His skin was still warm though, and she recoiled in sudden revulsion. She looked around him but could see no sign of injury: there was no pool of blood, no gunshot wound, no head trauma. The room showed no sign of any struggle either: the cushions on the sofa suite were casually arranged, the magazines on the side table were perfectly aligned in parallel rectangles—in fact, the place would have looked almost like a show home, except for the used glasses on the coffee table.

"Is he... is he dead?" came a whisper behind her.

Ellie turned to see Ava standing in the apartment doorway, peering nervously in. She rose slowly and stepped away from the body.

"Yes," she said with a sigh. "You'd better call the resort security."

Chapter Six

"You seem to have a knack for finding dead bodies, ma'am," said Detective Carson dryly as he sat next to Ellie on a bench outside the Ocean View Wing.

"Believe me, I don't go looking for them!" said Ellie. "Anyway, this isn't a murder, is it? He looks like he just had a heart attack."

"Hmm... I'm not ruling anything out at this stage," said Detective Carson. "We're treating the death as suspicious until proven otherwise—or at least until we get the results of the autopsy. The full report won't be for a few days, but we should have the preliminary results from the tox screen and general examination by tomorrow. In the meantime, I'd like to ask you some more questions. You said that you don't really know the dead man?"

"No," said Ellie. "At least, I only met him for the first time today. I happened to sit next to him in *Hammerheads Bar and Grill*. Oh, and I attended a cocktail workshop this afternoon, which happened to be run by his nephew."

Carson flipped back a few pages on his notepad. "Rob Saunders?"

"Yes, that's right." Ellie hesitated, remembering the conversation that she had overheard between Rob and his uncle. She hated the feeling of snitching on someone but if this was likely to be a criminal investigation, she had a duty to tell the police any information which might be useful. "I... erm... I overheard them talking earlier. Rob was trying to get his uncle to invest in a business idea of his, but Saunders was quite dismissive and brushed him off."

"Were they hostile with each other?"

"No, not hostile exactly but... well, Rob did seem quite resentful and frustrated with not being taken seriously," said Ellie.

"Hmm," said Carson, making notes in his pad. "And did you see Saunders with anyone else while you were in the restaurant?"

"Yes, like I told you, he had a business meeting with an alligator farm owner called Roy Mack."

"Right. And no one else?"

"Well, after Mack left, Saunders's wife joined him. She was a real—" Ellie broke off. She had been about to say "cow" but she amended it to: "She didn't seem very nice."

Carson raised his eyebrows. "What d'you mean by that?"

"She played a nasty prank on Ava—that's the waitress—over there..." Ellie pointed to where a young woman was sitting at another bench a few feet away. Ava had a blanket wrapped around her shoulders and was sitting with her head bowed, and her face looked haunted and scared. Ellie felt her heart go out to the girl. Finding a dead body wasn't a nice business and Ava had obviously been traumatized by the whole experience.

"Right, I spoke to her already." Carson gave the waitress a careless look, then turned back to Ellie and continued: "You said Tonya Saunders played a prank on her?"

"If you spoke to Ava, she would have told you about it already, wouldn't she?"

"I'd like to hear your version."

"Oh. Well, it was like a mean joke. Tonya kept asking for different soft drinks, and every time Ava brought the thing she'd asked for, Tonya would pretend that she asked for something else. She thought it was funny, and then when Sol, the head waiter, came to sort things out, she got him in trouble with her husband. I mean, I didn't actually *see* her put out a foot to trip Sol, but I'm sure that's what she did," said Ellie, pulling a face. "She knew it would make Sol spill the tomato juice on Saunders. He was furious, of course. He threatened to get Sol fired."

"Is that right?" said Carson with a gleam in his eyes. "And what did Sol do?"

"Oh, he was fantastic! He just remained patient and polite and calm, even though the Saunderses were so unpleasant. I mean, honestly, the way they were behaving, it would have provoked a saint to murd—oh!" Ellie covered her mouth. "Sorry, forget I said that! I didn't mean—I'm not suggesting that anyone thought of murdering Walter Saunders."

Carson didn't comment, although he scribbled something in his notepad. Ellie watched him nervously, silently cursing her wayward tongue.

"So then what happened?" asked Carson, raising his head again.

"Well, Saunders left to go back to his suite to change. Tonya followed him a few minutes later. Oh, she took his unfinished cocktail with her."

"This is the cocktail that he was drinking with Roy Mack, you said?"

"Yes, the Scorpion Bowl." Ellie described how the alligator farm owner had ordered the cocktails and added the repulsive dried scorpions. "Saunders obviously liked it better than he expected, since he asked his wife to bring his drink up to their suite. But wait…" Ellie sat up straighter. "I just realized: I didn't see it in the suite just now—the Scorpion Bowl, I mean. Have your men found it?"

Carson shook his head. "No sign of any cocktail."

"That's weird." Ellie frowned. "Tonya Saunders definitely took it up with her… Speaking of which, where's Tonya?" she asked suddenly, looking around. "I would have thought that she'd be with her husband."

"We're still trying to locate her at the moment," said Carson. "The Saunderses also own a yacht that's normally moored at the nearby marina. It's possible that Tonya has gone out on the boat and hasn't heard the news about her husband yet—"

He broke off as an officer approached them, holding something in a large evidence bag. He handed it to Carson and Ellie's eyes widened as she saw what was in the bag.

"That's the Scorpion Bowl!" she cried.

"Are you sure?" Carson asked.

She nodded, eying the ceramic tiki

bowl. "Definitely. That thing is pretty distinctive. Where did you find it?"

"It was shoved down inside one of those pots," said the officer, pointing to several large potted palms just outside the Ocean View Wing. "It was all bundled up in that," he added, pointing to the large piece of fabric wrapped around the bowl.

"Have you seen that before?" asked Carson, holding the bag up for Ellie to take a closer look.

She peered at the black cotton fabric through the clear plastic. She noticed a familiar logo embroidered in one corner, depicting a hammerhead shark swimming between the words "Bar" and "Grill."

"Oh, yes, that's Sol's apron. I saw it earlier this afternoon..." Ellie trailed off as she suddenly realized what her identification might imply. "I mean, I'm not sure if it's *Sol's* apron, exactly," she added hastily. "It looks like the one I saw him wearing, but it could just be a similar one." She knew, though, that it was unlikely, given that Sol had specifically told her he was the first staff member to get a sample of the new apron.

Carson gave her a long look, as if reading her mind, but he didn't comment. Instead, he waved the officer away and stood up, saying: "Well, thanks for answering my questions, Ms. Bishop. I'll have my men prepare a statement for you to sign. You're not going anywhere, are you?"

Ellie shook her head. "I'm staying at the resort until the new year."

"Good. Well, if this death turns out to be of natural causes, I guess we won't be talking again, but if this turns into a homicide investigation..." Carson trailed off ominously, then he gave Ellie a nod and turned and walked away.

Chapter Seven

"You're very listless this morning." Aunt Olive looked at Ellie in concern. "Is it because of what happened last night?"

Ellie gave her a wry smile. "You'd think finding a dead body wouldn't bother me by now. I've seen enough of them since arriving in Florida!"

"Mm... yes, there does seem to have been a spate of murders at the Sunset Palms recently. You could almost say that this is the deadliest beach resort in Florida!" said Aunt Olive, chuckling.

"Aunt Olive! It's hardly a laughing matter," said Ellie reproachfully. "A poor man is dead."

"Well, I'm not sure about the 'poor man' bit," said Aunt Olive. "From what you said, Walter Saunders sounded like the biggest wanker."

"*Aunt Olive!*" cried Ellie, really shocked now. "You're not supposed to know language like that!"

"Why? Because I'm in my sixties?" her aunt retorted. "We're not all twee little old ladies, you know. And I know a lot more colorful language than that. I used to date a chap in the Navy…" Aunt Olive gave a nostalgic smile. "Mm… what a dish he was… and he taught me how to swear in six languages. Would you like to hear how they insult people in—"

"Uh… never mind," said Ellie hastily. "And for heaven's sake, don't share any of your knowledge around Hemingway either! He's already picked up far too many embarrassing British insults."

As if on cue, there was a flurry of red

feathers and Hemingway landed on the back of Aunt Olive's chair.

"PEEKABOO!" he squawked, using one of his favorite words. Then he added: "YOU PLONKER!"

Ellie groaned as Aunt Olive burst into laughter. The parrot seemed to enjoy the effect he'd produced. He hooted excitedly, then hopped across to Ellie's chair and shuffled close to her. He lowered his head, exposing the naked skin between the feathers on the back of his neck.

"Looks like he wants a scratch," said Aunt Olive.

Ellie obliged for a few minutes, but when she stopped, the parrot nudged her again and lowered his head.

"Oh, Hemingway, I can't keep scratching you," Ellie said. She pointed to the plate in front of her. "My food has just arrived and it's getting cold."

The parrot cocked his head and looked

at her for a moment, then he said hopefully: "I BEG YOU?"

Aunt Olive raised her eyebrows "Did he just beg you to scratch his neck?"

Ellie guffawed. "No, I was trying to teach him to say 'I beg your pardon' last night—but he seems to have only picked up the first part."

"I BEG YOU?" Hemingway repeated. "I BEG YOU? I BEG YOU?"

"Argh! Oh, all right…" Ellie sighed and reached out to scratch the macaw's neck again.

She was glad that after a few minutes, something seemed to catch his interest and he flew over to a table on the other side of the terrace. She turned back to the plate in front of her with relief. They'd had a late start that morning so instead of rushing to make the last of the breakfast buffet, Aunt Olive had suggested having brunch at *Hammerheads Bar and Grill* instead. The menu there was bulging with tempting American breakfast options—although now, as Ellie looked down at the enormous stack of buttermilk pancakes drizzled with maple syrup, fresh blueberries, and fluffy whipped cream, she wondered how she was going to eat it all!

She was just picking up her knife and fork to start when they heard a commotion at the front of the restaurant. The place was relatively empty that morning so they were surprised by the noise. Ellie glanced over at the entrance, where Sol was behind the maître d' stand, facing two men. She felt uneasy as she recognized one of the men as Detective Carson.

"...I'm telling you, you've got the wrong man!" Sol was saying, his voice rising in agitation. "I had nothing to do with Mr. Saunders's death."

"That's not what we heard," said Carson. "His wife says you poisoned his cocktail."

"*What?*" Sol stared at the detective as if he'd gone crazy.

"Saunders's autopsy showed that he died of benzodiazepine poisoning—specifically diazepam," Carson added. "We tested the items found at the scene and we found significant amounts of diazepam in the remnants of liquid left in the ceramic cocktail bowl that Saunders had been drinking from."

"But... that's got nothing to do with me!" Sol protested.

Carson signaled to the officer with him, who held up a clear evidence bag similar to the one that Ellie had seen last night. But this time, it only contained the apron.

"Do you recognize this?" asked Detective Carson.

"It looks like my apron," admitted Sol.

"It was found wrapped around the

empty tiki bowl, which held Walter Saunders's cocktail."

Sol gaped at him. "How did it end up there?"

"That's what I'd like to ask you," said Carson. "You said it's your apron—so you were wearing it last night?"

"Well, yeah, until I gave it—" Suddenly, Sol clamped his mouth shut.

"Yes?"

"Uh… no, I took it off. I meant to say I was wearing it until I took it off," said Sol.

"When does the restaurant close?"

"Ten o'clock."

"And you were here until that time?" Carson glanced at the closed kitchen doors. "Can the other restaurant staff vouch for you?"

"Uh…" Sol shifted his weight. "Actually, I left early last night."

"What time?"

Sol told him and Carson looked at him sharply.

"That's about half an hour before Saunders's body was discovered," he said. "Why did you leave early?"

Sol hesitated. "I... I wasn't feeling well."

Carson raised his eyebrows. "And you went straight home? Anyone can verify that?"

Sol shook his head. "My neighbors work evening shifts, so they wouldn't have been home."

Carson was silent for a moment, then he said: "You're in charge of the bar here, aren't you?"

"That's right."

"So you normally mix all the drinks. You make up Saunders's cocktail?"

"No, this was a tiki cocktail so we ordered it over from the Tiki Bar by the pool. It was mixed there."

"And who served it?"

Sol hesitated again, then said, "One of our waitresses. Ava."

"Ah… yes, I spoke to her last night. She was pretty shook up about finding the body. She says, though, that *you* handed her the Scorpion Bowls from the bar."

"Paolo at the Tiki Bar brought them across and gave them to me. I called Ava over and got her to take the drinks to the table."

"So you could have added a little something extra to Saunders's drink when it was 'in transit,'" said Carson.

"But why would I?" demanded Sol. "Why would I want to murder Walter Saunders?"

"Witnesses say there was a scene here in the restaurant yesterday afternoon between you and the victim. You had to intervene when Saunders and his wife got into a fight with one of your waitresses."

"There was no fight," said Sol. "They were bullying her and I stepped in, that's all. It's not the first time that's happened and I'm used to dealing with situations like that."

"Well, maybe this time you decided you were sick and tired of situations like that. Maybe you thought it was time these rich folks paid for the way they treated everyone like trash," said Carson provocatively.

"You think I committed murder just because a customer was rude to me? Man, every waiter out there would be a criminal suspect if that was the case!"

"Saunders wasn't just rude. He threatened to have you fired."

Sol shrugged. "It was just hot air. Rich folk—as you call it—say that kind of thing all the time. They like to show that they've got power; it's like someone always wanting to have the last word.

But it doesn't really mean anything. They're like kids having a tantrum. You just soothe their egos and move on."

"Oh yeah? So then how come Saunders's wife is claiming that you poisoned his drink? She maintains that you deliberately spiked his cocktail to get revenge."

"That's... that's crazy!" Sol burst out.

"Where were you really last night?" Detective Carson asked abruptly.

"What do you mean?" asked Sol, suddenly looking wary. "I told you—"

"You're lying. I spoke to some of the other staff at the restaurant earlier this morning. They say you left suddenly in the middle of the evening shift and never came back. But it wasn't because you were sick. You looked fine, they said."

"I... I had something to do," mumbled Sol.

"And what was that?"

"It's... I..." Sol stammered. Ellie was surprised to see a flare of panic in his eyes. He looked around the restaurant as if searching for answers. "It's got nothing to do with Walter Saunders," he said at last.

"That's not what I asked," said Carson evenly. When Sol remained stubbornly silent, he said: "I think you'd better come down to the station with us—"

"No!" Ellie burst out, jumping up from her seat and rushing over to join them. "This is bonkers! You can't seriously be suspecting Sol of murder?"

Detective Carson glowered at her. "Ms. Bishop, I know you've been some help to the police in the past, but this time I must ask you to keep out of this."

"But I know Sol!" cried Ellie. "I know he would never murder anyone."

"It's all right, Ellie," said Sol gently.

"No, no, it's wrong!" Ellie insisted. She looked at Carson earnestly. "I'm one of the witnesses who was in the restaurant yesterday. Why didn't you ask me about it?"

"I already spoke to you last night, when we came to secure the crime scene," said Carson. "I don't need to ask you any more questions right now."

"Yes, but you didn't ask me about what happened earlier, here in the restaurant! I was here—I saw everything. I can tell you exactly what Walter Saunders said and how he treated Sol… and the waitress, Ava."

"If I want to speak to you again, I know where to find you," said Carson curtly.

"Also, your accusation doesn't make sense," Ellie rushed on. "You're saying that Sol's motive was revenge for how Saunders treated him. But you're also saying that he tampered with Saunders's cocktail much earlier, just after it was delivered from the Tiki Bar and before he passed it on to Ava to serve. Well, that's just stupid and illogical! How can Sol have spiked the drinks *then* because of a motive that didn't even exist yet? At that stage, Saunders's wife hadn't even arrived and the trouble with her prank and Ava hadn't even happened... so Sol would have had no reason to want to poison Saunders!"

Carson's mouth tightened and he flushed with anger. Ellie realized belatedly that bluntly criticizing his detective abilities wasn't going to get on his good side and help her case! She cursed her wayward tongue again and started to apologize, but Carson cut her off:

"As I said—if I want your *amateur* opinion, I know where to find you," he said through gritted teeth. "Now, if you'll excuse me, I've got a homicide investigation to run. Good day, ma'am."

Before she could think of how to reply,

Carson led Sol out of the restaurant, followed by the uniformed officer. Feeling angry and helpless, Ellie could do nothing but stand and watch them leave.

Chapter Eight

"Never mind, poppet," said Aunt Olive, patting Ellie's hand when she finally sat down again. "Sometimes the way in is not through the front door."

"What d'you mean?"

"Well, you might get better results if you speak to someone above Detective Carson… and we know someone who is very good friends with the county sheriff," she added with a wink.

"Of course!" cried Ellie. "Why didn't I think of that? Mr. Papadopoulos! Yes, I'm sure he'll hear my side of things." She sprang up from her seat. "Thanks,

Aunt Olive!"

She gave her aunt a peck on the cheek and rushed out of the restaurant. She hurried to the lobby and went up to the reception counter to ask for the resort owner. He'd told them several times that she and her aunt were considered VIPs at the resort and encouraged them to ask for him any time. *Well, I'm exercising that privilege now*, thought Ellie. A few minutes later, she was shown into a spacious office with a view of the resort's landscaped gardens. Mr. Papadopoulos himself was sitting behind an enormous executive desk. As usual, he was wearing his trademark white linen suit and his large, well-groomed moustache was twirled neatly on either side of his nose.

He looked up from signing some papers as Ellie was shown in and said: "Ah, Ellie, how nice to see—"

"Oh Mr. Papadopoulos, you can't let them arrest Sol!" Ellie burst out, rushing toward his desk.

"Arrest Sol? What do you mean?" he asked, looking bewildered.

"Detective Carson... the police... they came for Sol and took him away to the station. I was there; I saw it!"

"You saw them arrest him?"

"Well, no, not exactly," Ellie admitted. "They were taking him away for further questioning. But I can see that they're going after him for the murder of Walter Saunders and I don't want him to be arrested and charged for something he didn't do!"

Mr. Papadopoulos frowned. "Detective Carson spoke to me this morning and said that he would be questioning members of the resort staff, but he promised me that he would be discreet. I certainly didn't give him permission to march staff off the premises in front of guests!" He gave Ellie a reassuring look. "Don't worry, after we speak, I will call

Mike—Mike Gaskin—he's the county sheriff and he's a personal friend. I understand that they need to question people as part of the investigation, but I will make sure that my staff are treated with respect and consideration."

"But what about Sol?" asked Ellie. "You'll speak to Detective Carson, won't you, and tell him that they're wrong to suspect him?"

Mr. Papadopoulos sighed and indicated one of the chairs facing his desk. "Please… sit down."

Ellie perched on the edge of the seat.

"My dear, this is a homicide investigation and it's important that we let the police do their work. They have specific lines of inquiry that they need to follow up and we can't interfere with that. In Sol's case, it is true that there are some unexplained points, such as his unexpected departure from the restaurant yesterday evening. That is not his usual behavior at all and unless Sol can offer a satisfactory explanation, it's reasonable of the police to be suspicious."

"But… what does it matter if he was away from the restaurant last night?" asked Ellie, confused. "I thought Saunders was killed by poisoning? That's what Detective Carson said. He said it was in the Scorpion Bowl cocktail that Saunders was drinking."

"Yes, that's right. They found high concentrations of diazepam in the ceramic tiki bowl. Diazepam is the drug found in Valium," Mr. Papadopoulos explained. "It's fairly safe on its own but when mixed with alcohol, it can trigger lethal side-effects, such as respiratory failure."

"Is that what happened to Walter Saunders?"

Mr. Papadopoulos nodded. "Yes, essentially. Your breathing slows down so much that you can't get enough oxygen in your blood and then your heart stops. But the person wouldn't necessarily realize what's happening because they feel very drowsy. It's a common reason for deaths from accidental overdose, sadly. People don't listen or don't understand when they're told not to mix alcohol with diazepam. Of course, in this instance, it looks like someone mixed diazepam into Walter Saunders's cocktail on purpose. And given that he already had a heart condition, it didn't take much to produce a fatal overdose."

"But if the poison was in his cocktail, anyone could have put it in there," Ellie pointed out. "Aside from Sol, there was also Saunders's wife, Tonya, who had access to his drink. She was sitting right next to him at the table *and* she carried the cocktail up to his room later. And then there's his business partner, Roy Mack."

"Roy Mack? The owner of Groovy Gator Farm?" said Mr. Papadopoulos.

Ellie nodded. "Yes, before his wife joined him, Saunders had a meeting with Mack. I was sitting at the table next to them and I saw the whole thing. They were talking about cocktails and Mack insisted that they have a Scorpion Bowl each. In fact, he even added something to Saunders's drink. I saw him do it."

"What did he add?"

"Oh, it was a creepy dried scorpion. He had a bag of them. He seemed really into their 'health benefits.'"

"Ah, right—Manchurian scorpions? Yes, Roy Mack came to see me recently and we struck a deal to stock some things from the alligator farm in the resort gift shop. It was mostly items made from gator hide and some jewelry made from gator teeth, but I remember him showing me a packet of those scorpions. He thought they'd be a popular novelty item for tourists. I passed on them though." Mr. Papadopoulos looked at Ellie intently. "Are you suggesting that Mack added a poisoned scorpion to Saunders's drink?"

"Well... I suppose it could have been poisoned, although I saw him put a similar scorpion in his own drink as well," Ellie said. "But that could have been a sort of cover, couldn't it? Like, he had one himself, to show that they were fine—but in fact, the one that Saunders had was poisoned."

Mr. Papadopoulos looked unconvinced. "And was the one that was put in Saunders's drink taken from a different place?"

"No, they all came out of the same packet," Ellie admitted. "In fact, Mack let Saunders pick out his own scorpion himself, so unless Mack had poisoned them all, he couldn't really know which one Saunders would pick. But if he *did* poison them all, then his own scorpion would have been toxic too, so… hmm…" Ellie frowned. "I guess that doesn't really work."

"In any case, why would Roy Mack want to murder Saunders?" asked Mr. Papadopoulos.

"Oh, I heard them talking about the business—the alligator farm. Saunders was complaining about inconsistencies in the accounts and he said he was going to personally visit the farm and do an audit of everything. So maybe Mack wanted to get rid of Saunders before he flushed out any illegal activity at the farm," Ellie suggested.

"Did Roy Mack seem worried about Saunders's threat?"

"No, not really," Ellie admitted. "He got a bit indignant when he thought Saunders was accusing him of fraud, but he seemed perfectly happy for Saunders to go over to the farm and check everything. They'd arranged to meet at ten the next day—that's this morning," amended Ellie.

She couldn't believe that less than twenty-four hours had passed since she'd overheard that conversation. It seemed like it was already days ago!

"Anyway, if it's not him, there's still the wife… and also Saunders's nephew," she added, remembering. "He had a motive too."

"Do you mean Rob Saunders?" said Mr. Papadopoulos in surprise. "What motive could he have?"

"Oh, I… erm… overheard them talking as well," said Ellie, flushing slightly and hoping that Mr. Papadopoulos didn't think she was spending all her time going around snooping on other guests' conversations! "Rob wanted his uncle to invest in a business idea of his and Saunders wouldn't do it. Rob seemed really angry and resentful that his uncle would invest in 'random strangers' but wouldn't give his own nephew any support."

"Hmm. Detective Carson did tell me that, in her statement, Tonya said Rob Saunders was with her husband when she arrived back in their suite yesterday evening," said Mr. Papadopoulos. "She said they were discussing some kind of business, but she wasn't really paying attention. She just put the Scorpion Bowl on the coffee table in front of her husband, then went to the bathroom to freshen up before heading out again. She says Rob was still with Saunders when she left the room."

"Which makes him the last person to see Saunders alive!" said Ellie. "That's significant, isn't it?"

"Yes, but once again, what motive would Rob have?" asked Mr. Papadopoulos.

"Well… maybe… maybe Rob decided that if his uncle won't invest in his business idea, he could get hold of the money by killing Saunders and getting his inheritance instead."

"Hmm… well, Rob does stand to inherit the majority of his uncle's fortune," said Mr. Papadopoulos thoughtfully. "The details of Walter Saunders's will are not known yet, but it's generally believed that a large portion of the fortune is held in a trust which goes to Rob, as Saunders didn't have any children of his own."

"Really? I would have thought that as Saunders's wife, Tonya would have been entitled to most of his estate," said Ellie, with interest. "But anyway, the point is, don't you think all these people have much more reason to murder Saunders than Sol does?" insisted Ellie. "Their potential motives make much more sense than Sol killing Walter Saunders, just to 'get even' for a bit of customer rudeness."

Mr. Papadopoulos sighed. "I agree,

but there are other things which complicate Sol's situation." He hesitated, then added, "I know you care deeply for Sol so I will share something with you in confidence: Sol has a past record and that is what the police have honed in on."

Ellie stared at him. "What d'you mean by 'past record'? A criminal record?"

"Yes. He was involved with a local carjacking gang in his late teens and was arrested while stealing a car to take to the chop shop."

"What's a chop shop?"

"It's a place used by car thieves where the vehicles are dismantled very quickly, so that they can't be traced or found. The stripped parts are then sold."

"Sol was involved in that?" said Ellie in dismay.

"Well, he was only sixteen, I think, and he'd gotten in with a bad crowd. Given Sol's age and lack of criminal history, the court ruled it a first-time misdemeanor offense and decided to go easy on him. They sentenced him to probation and community service work. However, because auto theft is a third-degree felony in Florida, it does mean that he was left with a criminal record."

"The police told you this?"

"Sol told me himself," said Mr. Papadopoulos. "When we hired him, we did the usual background checks, of course, but we wouldn't necessarily have uncovered the record, because minors can have their records sealed. However, Sol made a clean breast of things. He decided that he wanted to be upfront from the beginning and not have it hanging over him. I was impressed by his honesty, and rather than putting us off hiring him, it was what secured him the job." Mr. Papadopoulos made a rueful expression. "However, from the police's point of view, he is someone who *does* have a criminal record."

"But it was so long ago!" protested Ellie. "I mean, Sol is in his—what—fifties? So that's over thirty years ago. Besides, surely there's a big difference between teenage car theft and murder?"

Mr. Papadopoulos inclined his head. "I agree with you, my dear, and I will certainly speak to the county sheriff on Sol's behalf. And the resort will support Sol in any way he needs: we'll make sure that he gets a good defense lawyer and we'll cover all legal fees. But in the meantime..." He reached across the table and patted Ellie's hand. "I know it's frustrating, but I think we need to leave the investigation to the police."

Chapter Nine

"Come along, poppet!"

Ellie looked up from the magazine she had been listlessly flipping through and turned to Aunt Olive, who had just come out of her bedroom. "Where are we going?"

"To the marina."

"The marina? Why?"

"I rang Earl a bit earlier to see if he's free this afternoon. He is, so I've organized for him to take us fishing!"

"Oh." Ellie tried to inject some enthusiasm into her voice.

The fact was, at any other time, she would have been excited at the idea of a fishing trip. She hadn't had a chance yet to go out on any boat trips in the Gulf and she'd often heard that fishing was one of the top activities for a vacation in Florida. Plus, she was keen to get to know Earl Stone better. He was a local boatman famous both for his wide knowledge and his unusual "loner lifestyle." He also happened to have the kind of rugged good looks and charisma which had caught Aunt Olive's eye.

When Ellie had first arrived in Florida, she'd gone into a frenzy of worry when she'd found her aunt's villa empty with no explanation of where she had gone. As it turned out, Aunt Olive, in her typical reckless and carefree way, had simply gone off with Earl for an impromptu three-day boat trip. Since then, Aunt Olive had continued seeing Earl from time to time, but Ellie had usually excused herself from their trips, as she didn't want to feel like a third wheel.

Now, she tried to get excited at the prospect of getting out on the water at last. It was hard to pull herself out of the gloom she had sunk into after what had happened with Sol. And a phone call with Blake hadn't improved her mood either. The handsome doctor had called her that morning after hearing about Walter Saunders's murder on the resort grapevine. He'd wanted to check that she was OK and also to apologize again for cancelling their date. But although Blake had sounded sincere, Ellie had noticed that he was cagey when she tried to ask him again about why he'd cancelled:

"So... did everything go OK last night?"

"Uh... yeah... yeah, it was fine."

"Did you get done what you had to do?" Ellie had asked, hoping to prompt him to give more details.

"Uh... pretty much."

Ellie had bitten back a growl of frustration and said with forced brightness: "Well, I'm free tonight. Maybe we could try dinner again—"

"Uh... not tonight," said Blake quickly. "Sorry, Ellie. I'm... I'm really tired. Burning the candle too hard at the clinic, I think," he said with a weak laugh. "I'm … uh… I'm just going to have a quiet night in, I think. Sorry... You don't mind, do you?"

"Oh. No... of course, not," said Ellie, swallowing her disappointment. She'd waited to see if Blake would suggest another night instead and, when he didn't, she'd eventually said goodbye after a few more words of stilted conversation.

Now Ellie felt the mixture of hurt and puzzlement fill her again. What was going on? Why was Blake acting so strange? Two nights ago, he had seemed as eager as she was to spend more time together—what had changed?

Maybe she was being too hard on him. After all, doctors worked long hours and she knew that Blake was often on-call and disturbed in the night by guest emergencies. Maybe he really *was* just tired, and the reason he sounded so uncommunicative was simply due to stress and fatigue. *A lot of people get cranky when they feel tired,* she told herself. *And although Blake seems like the most easygoing guy in the world, even "nice guys" have bad days sometimes, right?*

"Hello? Earth to Ellie! Are you there, poppet?"

Ellie started guiltily as she realized that her aunt was still standing next to her, waiting expectantly.

"Sorry, Aunt Olive." She gave a wan smile. "I'm not sure I feel like a boat trip.

Why don't you and Earl go—"

"Ohhh no! I'm not going to accept your excuses this time, young lady," said her aunt. "It'll do you good to get away from the resort a bit. There's no point sitting around here, brooding all day. That's not going to help Sol either."

"I'm not brooding!" protested Ellie.

Aunt Olive just gave her a look.

"Oh... all right," said Ellie with a sigh, getting up from the table and going obediently to her room.

She changed into a cotton button-up shirt and a pair of denim Bermuda shorts, slathered sunscreen over her skin, then tied her wayward curls back in a neat ponytail. Grabbing her sunglasses and a few other necessities, she hurried out to join her aunt, who was waiting for her by the front door.

Aunt Olive was wearing white Capri pants, a hot pink top, and an enormous, wide-brimmed, floppy hat atop her grey curls. Along with her diamante designer sunglasses and her red lipstick, she looked more like a movie star about to board a luxury yacht than someone going fishing. Ellie saw other resort guests eying them curiously as they walked toward the main resort tower.

As they entered the lobby, they were met by Mojito the resort cat, who trotted up to them and rubbed herself against their legs. Ellie bent automatically to pat the sleek black feline just as Aunt Olive said:

"Ah! What perfect timing. Earl asked me to bring Mojito along."

"He what?" Ellie looked up at her aunt in surprise. "He wants us to take the cat to the marina?"

Aunt Olive nodded. "Mojito used to belong to him, didn't you know? She used to be a 'ship's cat.' Earl found her as an abandoned kitten at the marina and rescued her. She lived on board his yacht for years and used to sail with him everywhere."

"Wow," said Ellie, looking down at the cat, who was purring happily, her eyes narrowed with pleasure as Ellie stroked her. "So how come she's living at the Sunset Palms now?"

"Oh, Earl got worried that being cooped up on a yacht all the time wasn't the best thing for her. He thought she'd have a better life on land. Mr. Papadopoulos is a good friend of his and you know how much Mr. P loves animals, so he was very happy to take Mojito in. But Earl still pops by to see the little puss whenever he can, and he takes her out with him for short trips sometimes. She loves the marina and she's still got her sea legs… or sea paws, I should say," said Aunt Olive with a wink.

Ellie shook her head. "Cats always seem to manage to get the best of both worlds, don't they?"

Aunt Olive went up to the reception counter to explain what they were doing and they were presented with Mojito's carrier. The black cat's eyes lit up as soon as she saw the carrier and she needed no urging to climb in, meowing excitedly the whole time. By the time they reached the marina, Ellie was beginning to share in the cat's excitement. As she stepped out of the car, she paused to take a deep breath, her spirits lifting as she took in the clear blue sky and the open docks around her. It was hard to feel down when you could feel the sea breeze on your face and see the sun sparkling on the water.

"It's good to see a smile back on your face, poppet," said Aunt Olive. "I told you coming was a good idea."

"You're right, as usual, Aunt Olive," said Ellie with a rueful smile. "And I *am* excited to go on a boat at last! I mean, a '*real*' boat—not one of those cross-channel ferries to France. That hardly feels like you're sailing."

Aunt Olive chuckled. "Well, you're going to get a 'proper' boating experience all right. Earl has a sportfishing yacht, designed for heading out to deep water and coping with rough weather. You could even live in it, out in the open ocean, for days—like we did on my first trip out with him."

"You mean, the time you didn't tell anybody where you were going and I thought you'd been abducted?" said Ellie reproachfully.

Aunt Olive ignored her words and continued cheerfully: "I'd been on several cruise ships, but I'd never lived on such a small vessel before. It was more comfortable than I expected. It's amazing what facilities you can fit on a boat."

"Do you really have proper kitchens and bathrooms and everything?"

"Oh yes. But they're not called

'kitchens and bathrooms.' If you're going sailing, poppet, you'd better learn the proper terms! The place where you prepare food is called the galley and the bathrooms are called heads."

"Heads?" Ellie furrowed her brow. "Why on earth are they called 'heads'?"

"I think it's a navy term. I researched this for a book once, and from what I can remember, it came from the old days, before there was modern plumbing. The sailors would relieve themselves at the front of the ship, beside the forward-most part, which protruded beyond the bow. That was called the 'head'—maybe because that was where the figurehead used to be hung. It was where water could easily wash the waste away; plus, in the days when ships relied on sails and wind power only, it was also the best place for the wind to carry odors away."

"Eww," said Ellie, wrinkling her nose at the thought. "You mean they just went to the toilet over the side of the ship?"

Aunt Olive shrugged. "Life was rougher in those days. Besides, there were only men on board then, so I suppose they weren't so fussed about privacy."

"OK, so the kitchen is the 'galley' and the bathroom is the 'head'... and the bedroom is the bunk, right?" asked Ellie, eager to have guessed something herself.

"No, actually, the bed itself is the bunk, but a bedroom on a boat is called a cabin or a berth—or a stateroom, if it's a larger room for the captain and special guests. On a big yacht, you might get a couple of staterooms leading off the companionway—that's the hatch which leads below deck—as well as some smaller berths for the crew. Oh, and don't forget the saloon, which is the communal living space for all passengers."

"I'm never going to remember all these terms," groaned Ellie. "It's like learning a whole new language."

"I haven't even started you on 'forward' and 'aft,' 'port' and 'starboard' yet," teased Aunt Olive. She lifted Mojito's cat carrier and started walking along the marina. "Right, let's see where Earl might be. He told me that we should be able to find him at Salty's Bar..."

Ellie followed as Aunt Olive led the way, looking around curiously. She'd heard a lot about the marina, but this was the first time she'd visited. The Sunset Palms Beach Resort was situated on one of the narrow barrier islands which hugged the coastline along this part of Florida. Each island was separated from the mainland by the Intracoastal Waterway, which connected via inlets to the Gulf of Mexico. The resort itself sat on the beach side of the island facing the Gulf, but the marina was situated on the opposite side, facing in toward the Intracoastal Waterway.

And while it was not as large or bustling as the more famous marina farther north at Clearwater Beach, the Sunset Palms Beach Marina had its fair share of fishing charters, sightseeing boats, dolphin tours, and even dinner cruises, as well as some personal watercraft rentals like jet skis. There was also a small row of shops and restaurants, and even a little pier from which you could fish for free or simply enjoy the beautiful view across the water.

Ellie followed her aunt as they walked down the boardwalk along the side of the main dock. In front of her were rows upon rows of boats, neatly lined up alongside the floating docks that stretched out like fingers from the main dock. She had never seen so many different types of boats gathered together. There were little aluminum fishing boats, rickety trawlers, and graceful sailboats, all the way up to power cruisers and luxury yachts that looked like something out of a Bond film.

"Look, there's Earl's boat," said Aunt Olive, pausing suddenly and pointing down the long floating dock next to them. Ellie turned to see a row of big motor yachts with streamlined bodies, each tapering to a pointed bow at the front. Some had multiple levels stacked one on top of the other above the deck, and they all looked sleek and powerful.

"Why don't you go on board first?" Aunt Olive suggested. "It'll give you a chance to look around. I'll go and find Earl."

"*MIAOW!*"

Aunt Olive looked down at Mojito, who was pressing her face against the bars of the cat carrier and looking eagerly at the boats lined along the floating dock. "So you want to go too?" She hesitated and looked around. "Well, I suppose it's safe enough. Earl says you're familiar with the marina anyway."

She set the carrier down and opened the door. Mojito darted out and gave herself a good shake, then immediately trotted toward the gangway leading down to the floating dock.

Aunt Olive chuckled. "Looks like Mojito knows the way. You just need to follow her—I'm sure she'll take you to Earl's boat."

"OK." Ellie watched her aunt continue down the boardwalk for a minute, then she turned and gingerly followed the cat down the gangway.

Chapter Ten

Ellie stepped off the gangway and took a few tentative steps along the floating jetty, unsure of her footing. But to her relief, although the long rectangular platform was obviously not permanently fixed, it didn't bob on the water or wobble like she expected. She walked slowly along, admiring the boats at closer range and keeping an eye on Mojito, who was trotting several yards ahead. The cat seemed totally at home in the marina surroundings, darting between the pilings and coils of rope, and ignoring the seagulls which wheeled overhead, calling raucously. Mojito made her way almost to the end of the floating dock, then paused next to a large yacht moored alongside. Without a backward glance, she hopped onto the swim platform at the rear of the boat and climbed on board, disappearing from sight.

"Mojito! Wait!" called Ellie, hurrying after the cat.

She reached the yacht and looked at it in some surprise. Somehow, when she had thought of Earl's boat, she hadn't imagined anything like this sleek gleaming monster. She had imagined Earl's boat to have a rugged, weathered look—something resembling the vessel that had carried Roy Schneider's sheriff and his team of shark hunters out to sea in the movie *Jaws*, perhaps. But this boat looked like it had glided straight out of a showroom. Everywhere she looked were gleaming white paint, glossy wood, and shiny metal trimmings. Then Ellie chided her silly imagination. After all,

Earl made his living offering private boat charters. Given the kind of guests that often stayed at the nearby resorts, it wasn't surprising that he would have a very nice boat: he would have to provide them with the kind of comfort they're used to.

Still, this is the height of luxury, Ellie thought as she stepped carefully on board. There were white padded leather seats on the rear deck, where you could sprawl in your bikini and play out your Bond-girl fantasies. There was a fridge and icemaker and even what looked like a small makeshift whirlpool tub! When she stepped inside the saloon, she saw that it was even bigger inside than it looked from the outside, with a large L-shaped settee in cream leather and high-gloss cherrywood cabinetry all around. There was a miniature kitchen—*no, a galley*, Ellie reminded herself—with counter and bar stools, and beyond it, she could see a hatch door with steps leading farther below deck.

Ellie hesitated, then descended the steps. After all, Aunt Olive had said she was free to explore as much as she liked, and she was fascinated to see how everything had been redesigned and adjusted to fit into the dimensions of the boat. At the bottom of the steps, she found herself in a short, narrow corridor. *The companionway,* she reminded herself. *And these doors must lead to the staterooms.* There were two doors on either side of the companionway, and a further one at the end, which was slightly ajar. Ellie walked over to this and poked her head through the door.

Wow, she thought. It was a big room, shaped to fit the pointed front end of the boat, and it was dominated by a sumptuous queen bed facing the door. Ellie looked around, taking in the expensive upholstery and polished wood cabinets. She'd had no idea that rooms on a boat could be this luxurious! There was another hatch door on the other side of the room, through which Ellie could see the gleam of a mirror. *The en suite bathroom,* she guessed. *Or actually, "en suite head,"* she corrected herself, smirking and pleased at remembering the new terms she had learned. Eager to see what it looked like, she went across and stepped through the connecting doorway. She found herself in a spacious bathroom modified to fit the shape of the boat, complete with shower, vanity unit, wall cabinets, and toilet.

Hmm... I wonder if the cabinets are full size? she thought, reaching out to open the mirrored cabinet door above the sink.

The shelves were shallower than what she was used to, but they seemed to hold an impressive number of things: toothpaste and soaps, cotton balls and toilet paper, and several boxes of pills. The boxes were neatly arranged with their sides lined up in perfect ascending order of height, and Ellie noticed one box with "Valium (Diazepam)" clearly printed on the side, sandwiched between a box of Tylenol and another of Pepcid Complete. She thought with some surprise that she hadn't expected Earl Stone to be the type to take Valium!

A noise outside brought her out of her thoughts and Ellie suddenly remembered Mojito. She hadn't seen the cat since coming aboard and she wondered where the little feline had gone. She smiled as she wondered if Mojito had joined her in the master stateroom and was making herself comfortable in her old spot on Earl's bed! Ellie was just about to step back through the connecting doorway when she froze.

There were voices outside... talking and breathy giggles... the sound of footsteps... people entering the stateroom... the rustling of fabric... Ellie peeked around the side of the connecting doorway and her eyes widened as she saw that, rather than Mojito, a man and a woman were lying on Earl's bed. They were tumbled on top of the covers, locked in a passionate embrace. The woman was giggling as the man tried to undo the buttons on her shirt, and saying:

"...you're not usually so slow! Aww... what's the matter, poopie-pie? Was last night too much for you? Are you feeling a widdle tired?"

"Oh no, not when I look at you, my cutie patootie..."

Ellie jerked back into the en suite head and wondered what to do. Who on earth were they? What were they doing on Earl's boat? Should she step out and reveal herself? Or should she just wait and hope that they might leave soon...? She winced as she heard more baby-talk and giggling coming from the room outside.

"...ooooh! Stop, poopie-pie! That tickles... hahaha!"

"I wuv my sexy snookums... I wuv your wotally worgeous boobies..."

Ellie cringed and groaned silently. Oh no, she'd die of embarrassment if she had to stay here listening to this couple's mushy love-making!

Maybe I can creep past without them noticing, she thought. They sounded so engrossed in each other, they probably wouldn't even hear her tiptoeing past. Taking a deep breath, Ellie slipped out of the hatch doorway and stepped back into the stateroom. She was relieved to see that the couple were still dressed. *Thank God for small mercies!* Carefully, she began creeping around the bed. The deep, plush carpet underfoot muffled the sound of her feet and she moved as unobtrusively as she could. She was just rounding the corner of the bed and thinking she was going to make it, when the couple rolled over suddenly.

The woman sat up astride the man, raising an arm and whooping like a cowboy riding a bucking bronco. Then she froze with her arm in midair and her mouth hanging open.

Ellie froze as well.

They gaped at each other.

"Who the hell are you? What are you doing on my boat?" the woman snarled, springing off the bed.

"Your... your boat?" stammered Ellie.

Then she stared even more as she suddenly recognized the woman. It was Tonya—Walter Saunders's wife! And judging from the scene in front of her, the woman didn't seem to be busy mourning her dead husband. Even as she had the thought, she saw Tonya recognize her too and an uneasy expression flicker across the other woman's face.

"Yeah, this is the *Saunders Spirit*. My *private* boat," Tonya snapped. "And you're trespassing!"

"I... I'm sorry," Ellie stammered. "I thought... I thought it was a charter boat—"

"A charter boat?" said Tonya, curling her lips. "Honey, does this look like some tourist charter boat to you?" she asked, her voice dripping sarcasm as she gestured around the stateroom.

Ellie looked at the luxurious furnishings and flushed. "Well, no, I mean... I thought it was outfitted especially for guests... and... and the cat jumped straight on the boat like she knew it—"

"What cat?"

"The resort cat... Mojito... she used to belong to the charter boat owner and I thought she was leading me..." Ellie trailed off. Even to her own ears, she sounded confused and lame.

"You followed me on purpose, didn't you?" Tonya said suddenly "That's right,

I recognize you! You're that little snitch who was at the restaurant! What are you trying to do now? Spy on me?"

"No!" said Ellie.

"Oh yeah? Then what are you doing in my bedroom? And you were in my private head just now, weren't you? What were you doing in there?"

"I... I told you, I thought it was a charter boat... and... and they said it was OK for me to look around—"

"You liar! You were in here, trying to snoop on me! You're a filthy little sneak but don't think you're going to get away with it!"

Ellie took a deep breath, regaining her composure. She had been surprised and put on the back foot, but now the woman's aggressive manner was beginning to annoy her. Even if she had inadvertently trespassed on the boat, there was no need for Tonya to be this aggressive!

"Look, I'm sorry. I didn't realize. It was an honest mistake, OK?" she said, looking the woman straight in the eye. Then, with great dignity, she turned and left the room.

Ellie made her way back up the companionway and onto the deck. She could hear Tonya behind her. The woman followed her to the edge of the deck, and stood and watched until Ellie had climbed off the boat. Mojito popped her head out from behind a piling just as Ellie stepped back onto the floating dock.

"There you are! You got me in a lot of trouble, you know," muttered Ellie, scowling at the cat. Mojito blinked at her innocently.

Ellie paused for a moment, unsure what to do. She looked at the other boats moored around her. She wasn't sure which one was Earl's boat—and she didn't dare trust Mojito's judgement anymore either! Afraid of making the same mistake again and having to explain herself to yet another angry boat owner, Ellie decided the safest thing was to go back and find Aunt Olive.

"Come on," she hissed to Mojito, who trotted obediently after her as she turned and headed back up the long floating dock toward the gangway.

Tonya was still standing on the deck of her boat, watching Ellie with narrowed eyes, and as she walked away, Ellie could feel the woman's eyes boring like X-rays into her shoulder blades.

Chapter Eleven

Just as Ellie reached the gangway which joined the floating dock with the main marina, she met Aunt Olive coming in the opposite direction. Her aunt was accompanied by a tall, rugged-looking man in his sixties, with grey hair pulled back in a low ponytail and the kind of muscular arms normally seen in men half his age. Earl Stone was one of those men who seemed to become more attractive with age. Somehow, the lines etched into his face and at the corners of his eyes, crinkled from years of squinting in the sun, just enhanced his weather-beaten good looks.

Ellie had met Earl a few times since arriving in Florida, but still found him a bit of a mystery. He might have been able to tell you a wealth of knowledge and stories about the local area, but he told you very little about himself. *Maybe that's part of his appeal for a mystery author like Aunt Olive*, thought Ellie with a smile. Still, his "strong, silent type" act obviously didn't extend to Mojito! Earl crouched down and made a huge fuss of the cat who had given a *"MIAOW"* of delight as soon as she had seen him and had scampered up the gangway to meet him.

"Hello, poppet—did you enjoy having a look around Earl's boat?" asked Aunt Olive as she joined Ellie on the floating dock.

"I would have, if I'd actually found Earl's boat," said Ellie. "As it was, I found Walter Saunders's widow in the arms of another man instead!"

"Really?" said Aunt Olive, looking

thrilled. "Do tell!"

Quickly, Ellie recounted what had happened, while Earl played with Mojito next to them.

"So Saunders's wife is having an affair?" said Aunt Olive, her eyes sparkling. "Who was the man?"

Ellie shrugged. "I don't know. He didn't say a word. In fact, his whole manner seemed oddly... well, it was almost as if he was beneath her?"

"I hope you're talking literally," said Aunt Olive with a naughty smile.

"Aunt Olive!" said Ellie in exasperation.

"All right, all right..." Her aunt chuckled. "It sounds like he might be a crew member. Maybe the captain of the yacht? A billionaire like Saunders would have a full-time crew on his yacht and I can just see Tonya playing out a 'Lady Chatterley' fantasy."

"Whoever it was, it seems really poor taste," said Ellie. "I mean, her husband was only murdered yesterday!"

"Mmm," Aunt Olive agreed. "Tonya did sound like a little gold-digger, from what you'd told me, but this is pretty heartless, even for her. To be caught canoodling with another man the day after her husband is poisoned... But it's interesting that she was so scared when you walked in on them."

"Scared? Tonya didn't look scared—she looked bloody furious!" said Ellie.

"Ah... but a lot of the time, anger is a cover for fear," said Aunt Olive wisely. "Especially when people overreact about something."

Ellie thought about what her aunt had said and realized that she was right. Tonya Saunders's reaction had seemed a bit excessive at the time and now Ellie recalled the fleeting expression of fear that she had seen crossing the woman's face.

"But I don't understand—why should Tonya be afraid?" she asked. "I mean, I suppose it looks bad and it *is* shameful behavior, but I wouldn't have thought Tonya is the kind of woman to care much about gossip? If anything, I would have thought she's the type that loves attention and absolutely revels in being the subject of gossip!"

"Unless that gossip might be harmful to her in some way," said Aunt Olive.

"You mean, if people think she killed Saunders?" said Ellie, frowning.

"That's one reason. It certainly starts to make you wonder about possible motives when you learn that she's been unfaithful. But I also wonder if it might affect her position on the division of the estate. I get a feeling that a woman like Tonya always operates with money in mind," said Aunt Olive cynically. Then she patted Ellie on the arm. "Anyway, you can put it all out of your mind for now, dear. For the next few hours, all you're going to think about is bait and tackle and how to reel in a rod as fast as you can!"

Ellie followed her aunt and Earl down the floating dock, retracing her steps past the *Saunders Spirit*. There was no sign of Tonya now—she had obviously gone back down below deck—and Ellie couldn't help wondering what the woman was getting up to. Then she reminded herself of Aunt Olive's words and hastily put the woman from her mind.

When Ellie climbed aboard Earl's boat, moored a couple of slips beyond the *Saunders Spirit*, she looked around appreciatively. *OK, this is more like what I was expecting*, she thought. Although still a large, powerful boat with comfortable amenities, it was outfitted in a noticeably more modest way, with a lot less cream leather and polished teak wood everywhere, and no outrageous additions like a whirlpool tub!

She perched on one of the seats on the aft deck and watched as Earl untied the cleats and motored the powerful yacht back out of its slip and away from the floating dock. They moved smoothly out of the marina and into the narrow channel of the Intracoastal Waterway. There was a stiff wind that day, so that even in the sheltered waters of the Intracoastal, there were large ripples on the surface of the water, and the boat rocked a bit more than Ellie had expected.

"It's all right, you're safe," said Earl, looking down at where her hands were clenched on the rail running along the side of the boat.

Ellie gave him a sheepish smile, forcing herself to unclench her fingers. "Sorry. I haven't been on a proper boat before so it's all a bit new to me. I hope I won't get seasick."

"Oh, you'll be fine, poppet," said Aunt Olive. "We're not going offshore fishing so we won't be heading out to the deep waters of the Gulf."

Earl nodded. "Thought I'd start you off nice an' easy," he said to Ellie with a smile. "We'll be stickin' with inshore fishin' today."

"What's the difference?" asked Ellie.

"Distance... and depth. When you're fishin' inshore, you only go a few miles off the coastline. Water's usually no more than thirty meters deep. But that don't mean you don't get a decent catch," Earl added quickly. "Some of the best fishin' around Tampa Bay is in the inshore waters. Snook, mackerel, trout, tarpon, redfish, shark—"

"Shark!" said Ellie incredulously. "You can fish sharks?"

"Oh yeah. They don't call Tampa Bay the 'Shark Capital of the World' for nothin'! We've got some of the most shark-infested waters out there." Earl laughed at her expression. "Don't worry, we don't get many Great Whites in the Bay. But you can get a whole bunch o' other species, like Nurse sharks, Bull sharks, Black Tip, Lemon… all the way up to fifteen-foot monster Hammerheads. Shark fishin' is best in the warmer months though."

Aunt Olive leaned over and handed Ellie a pair of binoculars. "Here… have a look through these. You might be able to spot one."

"Really?" said Ellie with a mixture of apprehension and delight. She raised the binoculars to her eyes and scanned the water around them. "Well, at least you can stay safe from sharks if you just keep out of the water—unlike alligators! They seem to be everywhere on land, from what people tell me."

Earl chuckled. "Oh, there are gators here too."

"Alligators? In the waters here?" Ellie lowered the binoculars and looked at him in surprise.

"Yeah. It's not common but it happens. They pulled an eight-footer out of the marina at West Palm Beach a few years ago. That's on the other side of Florida, of course, but it could happen here."

"But isn't the Intracoastal Waterway salty? I thought alligators couldn't survive in salt water?"

"That's a myth," said Earl. "They're freshwater critters, but they can survive in salt water if they have to, for days at a time. You can find gators in all sixty-seven Florida counties, in any body of water. Just ask the FWC—that's the Florida Fish and Wildlife Conservation Commission." Then he smiled at Ellie, his eyes crinkling at the corners. "But don't let that scare you. Sure, we get gator attacks every year, but it's a fact that snakes, spiders, and even mosquitoes are more of a danger than anythin' else."

"But what do you do if you *are* attacked by a gator?" asked Ellie. "Is it true that you should run in a zigzag? I've heard a lot of the resort guests saying that."

Earl guffawed. "That's another myth. Gators can run in a zigzag, no problem— and a lot faster than you expect too!"

"What about poking them in the eye?" asked Aunt Olive. "I've read that that works."

"Well, if you're close enough to do that, you're probably in its mouth. If a gator is chompin' on you and you can think clearly enough to poke 'em accurately in the eye... sure, go for it," said Earl dryly.

Ellie laughed. She was beginning to see why her aunt found Earl so charming.

"So what are you supposed to do?

Play dead?" she asked.

"Oh, don't do that—or else you won't be playin' very long!" said Earl. "Best thing to do is to fight back. Give it everythin' you've got and then some. Scream, yell, smack it on the head, splash water... that might convince the gator you're not worth the trouble and it might let you go."

"But doesn't an alligator have really thick skin? Will it feel anything if you smack it?" said Ellie doubtfully.

"There are some sensitive spots. The snout, for example—there're a couple of receptors there—and yeah, the eyes are vulnerable if you can get to 'em." Earl leaned forward and wagged a finger. "But the best thing is not to get so close that a gator can grab you in the first place! And if you see a gator comin' for you, best thing is to skedaddle—in a straight line—as fast as you can."

"I'll keep that in mind," said Ellie with

a nervous laugh.

"MIAOW!"

They looked up to see Mojito's head peering down at them over the edge of the upper deck, where the cockpit was located. Ellie marveled at how the cat seemed so at home on the boat. Earlier, she had seen Mojito running along the gunwale, barely a few inches from the edge of the boat, scampering happily over the various ropes and cleats in the bow, climbing in and out of hatches, and leaning over the side rails to peer curiously at the waves rolling past. The mischievous feline seemed to be in her element and didn't even seem to notice the rocking motion of the boat as it powered through the water.

They headed steadily out until they reached the area just beyond the mouth of the Bay, where it merged with the open waters of the Gulf. Then Earl set up seven-foot spinning rods, and Ellie watched in fascination as he baited the hooks using fresh shrimp. He cast the rods expertly into the water, then, to Ellie's surprise, handed one of them to her.

"Oh! I've never fished before in my life," she protested.

Earl smiled at her, his eyes crinkling at the corners. "Always a first time."

"But I don't know what to do!"

"Don't worry, you'll learn. Just hold the rod and keep one hand lightly on the reel handle—that's right—and stay alert for any tug on the line."

Ellie gripped the rod tightly and stared nervously out at the water, bracing herself to pull back against something yanking the line any moment. When nothing happened after five minutes, however, she began to relax. When nothing happened after another five minutes, she looked at Earl quizzically.

"What's happened? Why aren't they biting?"

Aunt Olive burst out laughing. "Patience, poppet! You've barely got started. Fishing is a waiting game."

Chapter Twelve

Aunt Olive leaned comfortably against the side of the yacht, next to Ellie, and turned back to Earl.

"So you were telling us about the alligators... don't people keep them as pets? Surely they can't be that dangerous, then?"

"Yeah, people get 'em as babies, but they always end up having to rehome 'em when they grow bigger," said Earl in disgust. "Gators look kinda cute when they're small, but they're gators just the same. They're not like dogs. They're not gonna bond with you and learn to love you."

"I'm surprised you're allowed to have them as pets at all—aren't they endangered?" asked Ellie, distracted from watching her line.

"They used to be. Almost hunted to extinction at one point. But not anymore. After the government got tough with protection laws, the population's recovered. There are over a million gators living wild in Florida."

"*A million!*" Ellie gulped. "That many?"

"They're still on the threatened species list though, so under state law, you still need to have a permit to keep one."

"What if you find an alligator egg?" suggested Aunt Olive. "Can't you just take it home and hatch it?"

"You need a permit to take eggs from the wild," said Earl. "And the FWC regulates that real tight. There are only a limited number of permits per year and each permit only lets you harvest a certain number of eggs."

"I never realized you knew so much about alligators, Earl," said Aunt Olive.

The boatman smiled. "I thought about goin' into the gator farm business a few years back, so I did my homework. It's a tough industry to get into. The permits are only issued by the FWC and they're on a first-come, first-serve basis. The established gator farms always get 'em, so newcomers don't get permission from the state to collect eggs."

"Is that why you didn't do it? Because you couldn't get any eggs?" asked Ellie.

"Oh, you can still get eggs. You collect 'em from private land. There are private properties all over the state with gators nestin' on 'em. But it's a helluva cost. You gotta pay the landowners for access and then you gotta pay the government a severance tax too, for each and every egg you collect." Earl shook his head.

"It's not my kinda party."

"How many eggs would you usually find in a nest?" asked Ellie.

Earl shrugged. "Between twenty and fifty."

"So why can't you just get two adult alligators and keep them to make babies for you?"

Earl laughed heartily. "They just never breed as well as they do in the wild. That's why all gator farms still harvest eggs from the wild—they'd never be able to breed enough each year to supply the market for gator hide and meat."

"Do that many people really want alligator meat?" asked Ellie. "I wouldn't have thought it's that popular."

"Oh, you'd be surprised, poppet. It's a low cholesterol, low fat, high protein white meat," said Aunt Olive. "Chefs are always looking for the 'new' healthy gourmet ingredient."

Earl nodded. "There was a real trend for it a while back. A lotta restaurants in the Southern states serve it on their menu. Gator tastes pretty good."

"Yes, I know—I've had some," said Ellie with a smile. "'Gator bites' from the Snack Shack at the resort. I enjoyed them more than I thought I would. But I didn't think gator meat would be accepted in the mainstream?"

"Well, it *is* the hides that bring in the big bucks," Earl conceded. "Those fashion houses over in Europe pay a lot to get hold of the hide. Hey, if you're interested in this stuff, there's a gator farm near the resort that you could visit. They do tours; they can tell you a lot more about farmin' gators—"

"This isn't the farm owned by Roy Mack, is it?" asked Ellie suddenly.

"Yeah, that's right," said Earl, looking surprised. "Groovy Gator Farm. You know Mack?"

"Not personally. I happened to see him at the resort yesterday with Walter Saunders… you know, before Saunders was found dead. They were having drinks together at the table next to me. Are *you* friends with Roy Mack?" asked Ellie cautiously.

"Met him once or twice. You get to know the other players in the local tourism racket, but I wouldn't say we're friends," said Earl.

"What do you think of him? Is he generally… erm… respected in the industry?"

"What Ellie's really trying to ask with all her tiptoeing around is whether you think Mack could have murdered Walter Saunders," said Aunt Olive with a chuckle.

Ellie shot her aunt a reproachful look, but she was secretly pleased that the subject had been broached.

"Well, now…" Earl leaned back and

narrowed his eyes thoughtfully. "Hard to say with a man like Mack. Don't like him much myself. Always struck me as a loudmouth show-off, goin' on about booze and girls. He's the kinda guy who would pull off jackass stunts like tryin' to bite the head off a live cockroach, just to get a reaction—know what I mean? But maybe that's just the showman in him. He used to be on the circuit in downtown St. Pete; had a regular show doing a mix of stand-up comedy, magic tricks, daredevil stunts, you name it. He left it all behind when he went into the gator farmin' business, but maybe he misses the crowds. These showbiz types like the attention, right?"

"What about—" Ellie broke off as she felt the rod suddenly being yanked from her hands. She cried out and grabbed it as the reel spun furiously and the line screamed down the rod.

"You've got a fish!" squealed Aunt Olive. "Quick! Reel it in!"

"I... I'm trying!" gasped Ellie. She could barely hold on, never mind try to turn the reel handle. She gasped and staggered left and right, clutching the rod and trying to wind the reel. The line ran taut into the water and the rod bent in a U-shape as the fish pulled frantically.

"It's a fighter," said Aunt Olive admiringly.

"Reckon it's a drum," said Earl, squinting at the surface of the water and the wriggling shape just visible beneath the surface.

"A... a drum?" said Ellie breathlessly, still struggling with her rod.

"Red drum... also called red fish. One of the most common fish you find around here. Delicious grilled." He smiled at Ellie. "Real feisty too. Even experienced fishermen respect 'em 'cos they put up a good fight."

"Gr-great," said Ellie, still struggling

to hold on to the rod as it bent even more.

"Don't try to wind the reel when the fish is really pullin'," Earl told her. "Let him run with it, then as soon as you feel the line slacken, reel him in, as fast as you can. When he starts pullin' again, let it go. Let him exhaust himself... and eventually, he'll come boatside and we can haul him up."

Ellie tried to follow Earl's advice and, after a few attempts, she was delighted to find that she was starting to get into the rhythm of easing off when the fish was pulling and winding as fast as she could when she felt the line slacken. It was still a tough match and the water churned with foam as the fish splashed and fought. Soon the muscles in Ellie's arms were aching with the effort of holding the rod, and she was sweating and breathing hard.

Just when she thought she could no longer hold on, she saw a pale oval shape coming close to the boat. Sunlight glinted on the scales covering the streamlined body and Ellie saw the flick of tail fins.

"Oh! I see it! I see it!" she shouted in excitement.

"That's a red drum—a real beauty," said Earl, nodding with satisfaction. "Bring him closer to the boat…"

Ellie reeled even harder, then she flicked the rod backwards, trying to lift the fish out of the water. It was still wriggling and flailing madly, and she thought for a horrified moment that it was going to slip off the hook; then Earl leaned out over the side of the boat and caught the fish in a hand-held net. He swung the net into the boat and dropped the fish on the deck.

Ellie gasped with relief and lowered the rod, leaning against the side of the yacht to catch her breath. She felt exhausted—but wonderfully exhilarated too.

"I did it! I caught a fish!" she squealed to Aunt Olive, who gave her an indulgent smile.

Ellie hurried over to join Earl, who was crouched next to the net, and gazed at the fish he was holding in his hands. It had a beautiful copper sheen to its scales and there was a large black spot near its tail. She was puzzled to see Earl measuring it.

"What are you doing?"

"Checkin' the size. Gotta be bigger than seventeen inches, otherwise you gotta put it back." He smiled at her and made a thumbs-up sign. "It's twenty-one inches. Great catch."

Ellie looked at the fish, which was still flipping its tail and opening and closing its mouth. She felt a sudden stab of pity. "Can I still release it?" she asked.

Earl laughed. "Sure. If you want. Here you go." He leaned across and put the fish into her arms.

Ellie reeled back slightly, clutching the slippery body to her. The fish wriggled, still fighting, and she felt a flash of admiration for its spirit. She stood up and approached the side of the boat.

"Hang on! Let me get a picture!" cried Aunt Olive, grabbing her phone. She snapped a few shots of Ellie proudly holding her catch, then smiled with satisfaction. "Brilliant! I'll send one of these to your parents, poppet. Tell them that you caught your first Florida fish today!"

Ellie smiled, feeling that rush of achievement again. Then she turned and leaned over the side of the boat and gently tipped the fish out of her arms. It dropped into the water with a small splash and, with a flick of its tail, it was gone, back into the depths.

Chapter Thirteen

"I don't know about you, poppet, but I could really do with a nice, cool drink," Aunt Olive declared when they arrived back at the Sunset Palms Beach Resort. "Shall we sit in the lobby bar for a bit?"

They let Mojito out, dropped the cat carrier back at the reception desk, then made their way across to the bar. The lobby was buzzing today, with groups of people gathered amongst the potted palms or relaxing on the couches in the seating area. It looked like several tour groups as well as families had just arrived and were checking in. There was a loud hum of talk and laughter, with children running and playing between the adults, and bellmen trying to sort through all the luggage. It was a scene of happy chaos and Ellie smiled. She loved loitering in the lobby, people-watching and enjoying the general vacation atmosphere.

When they reached the bar, they found a small group of women clustered around one of the bar stools and, as they got closer, they saw that Rob Saunders was at the center of the group. At first, Ellie thought he was doing another of his cocktail workshops. Then she realized that the young man was simply trying to impress several female guests with his cocktail knowledge. There were lots of giggles and coy glances and playful touches on the arms and shoulders as the women flirted with him. Rob Saunders basked in the attention, flashing his brilliant white smile and oozing smooth charm.

"Hmm... a real ladies' man, that one," said Aunt Olive, eying him as they sat down at a table nearby.

"Yeah, that was the impression I got when I was doing the cocktail class," said Ellie. "He was really flirtatious and knew how to flatter the ladies." She watched him for a moment, then sighed and said, "First Tonya and now Rob... neither Walter Saunders's wife nor his nephew seem to be that upset about his death, are they? I mean, the man only died yesterday and she's already busy canoodling with another man and he's busy flirting with random girls."

"Well, they do say grief takes people in different ways. Perhaps distracting themselves is their way of coping," said Aunt Olive.

"It really makes you wonder though," mused Ellie. "You know what? I wish there was some way I could question Rob about his uncle's murder. Detective Carson doesn't seem to be doing anything other than trying to pin the murder on Sol! I'm sure there's something Rob's not telling—I wish I could just walk up to him and ask him about yesterday."

"Well, why don't you?" asked Aunt Olive.

Ellie looked at her aunt impatiently. "I can't. I'm not the police."

Aunt Olive waved a disdainful hand. "You don't need to be the police! You just need to use your imagination, dear. A good sleuth only needs resourcefulness and determination—and a willingness to step outside the boundaries a bit sometimes," she added with a roguish smile.

"What d'you mean?"

"Well..." Aunt Olive eyed Rob Saunders speculatively. The group of women around him had dispersed and the young man was alone now. He raised a cocktail glass to toast two girls sitting farther down the bar who giggled and whispered together, throwing coy looks at him over their shoulders. "Rob Saunders is obviously a bit of a Casanova. You're a young, pretty girl. You could use that to your advantage."

"What? You're not telling me to seduce him, are you?" cried Ellie.

"Oh, don't look so shocked. I'm not suggesting that you sleep with him," said Aunt Olive, clicking her tongue. "But a man like Rob... well, now, he'd be easy to interrogate if you know how to play him." She saw Ellie's expression. "Oh, come on, poppet! Calculated seduction is a time-honored tradition in intrigue and espionage! I know it's not politically correct to say this nowadays, but you can achieve a lot with a suggestive smile and a show of cleavage."

"Aunt Olive! You've just set the women's lib movement back fifty years or something!"

"Rubbish!" snorted her aunt. "A woman who knows how to use her feminine charms to get what she wants is the one who's truly empowered."

"Why can't I just go over and talk to Rob normally?" asked Ellie.

"Because he's much more likely to let his guard down if he thinks you're an empty-headed flirt and he's just trying to impress you."

"Well, I don't have the kind of 'feminine charms' needed anyway," said Ellie, throwing an envious glance at the voluptuous figure of a girl walking across the lobby.

"Oh, you just need to make the most of your assets," said Aunt Olive, turning to look at Ellie critically. She reached out suddenly and yanked Ellie's shirt out from where it was tucked into her Bermuda shorts.

"What are you doing?" hissed Ellie in surprise.

"Improving your arsenal," said Aunt Olive briskly.

She unbuttoned Ellie's shirt from the bottom and tied the two loose ends in a neat knot just under Ellie's breastbone, exposing her midriff. Then she unbuttoned the shirt from the top so that the collar was more open and pulled and tucked in several directions.

"There!" she said at last.

Ellie leaned over to look in the mirrored walls of the bar and was pleasantly surprised by her own reflection. Somehow, Aunt Olive's adjustments had turned her baggy, prim, button-up shirt into a stylish crop-top which enhanced her waistline and her bust. Her exposed midriff and open collar showed off just enough skin to be eye-catching, without being too sexual.

"You just need one more thing," said Aunt Olive, fishing in her handbag and retrieving a tube of lipstick. Before anyone could stop her, she'd applied the lipstick generously to Ellie's startled mouth.

"Perfect!" she said, sitting back and looking at Ellie with satisfaction

This time when Ellie looked in the mirror, she recoiled slightly. She normally favored lip glosses in pale pink shades and the sight of the big red pout on her face was almost frightening.

"Oh my God—I look like a clown!" she gasped.

"Nonsense!" said Aunt Olive. "There's nothing to match the power of a bold, red lip. Cleopatra used it, Queen Elizabeth I used it, Marilyn Monroe used it… You want to feel capable and confident? Wear red lipstick."

Ellie still wasn't convinced. But there was no arguing with Aunt Olive when she was in this mood.

"Well, go on!" said Aunt Olive, making a shooing motion with her hands.

"This is crazy! I'm not doing this," said Ellie.

Aunt Olive regarded her severely. "Do you want to help Sol or not?"

"Of course I do!"

"Well, wouldn't you rather give it a try, than sit here brooding about things?" Her aunt leaned forward. "Yes, it might be a bit silly and it probably won't work, but what have you got to lose?"

"But I can't just walk over and start flirting with Rob—"

"Why not?" Aunt Olive demanded. "If Rob was a girl and you had to walk over and pretend to be chatty and friendly, just so you could get information out of her—you wouldn't hesitate, would you?"

"Yes, but that's different—"

"What's the difference? This is just a disguise, an act. And you don't even have to do anything special. Just behave the way any normal girl would act if she were interested in a boy." Aunt Olive frowned at her. "You *do* know how to flirt, don't you, poppet?"

"I… yes… I mean, no… I don't… Look, this is ridiculous!" Ellie spluttered. She glanced around the lobby and lowered her voice. "Besides, what if… what if other people see and get the wrong idea?"

"What other people?" asked Aunt Olive in bewilderment. Then understanding dawned and she gave a sly smile. "Oh, you're worried about your handsome doctor, are you? Don't worry, if I see him in the lobby, I'll personally go over and explain the situation to him—"

"No, you will not!" said Ellie, horrified. "I don't want you saying a word of this to anyone."

"Well, if you hurry up, you'll be back before you know it, and no one needs to know a thing," said Aunt Olive sweetly.

Ellie hesitated, looking across at Rob Saunders again. Part of her felt the whole idea was too outrageous to even contemplate, but she had to admit that a tiny part of her was also excited by the challenge. She'd never done anything like this before. Could she pull it off? And her aunt was right: wasn't doing something proactive—even something as ridiculous as what Aunt Olive was suggesting—better than just sitting around, feeling frustrated and helpless by the whole situation?

Finally, she sighed. "Oh, all right. I'll give it a shot. But I'm not putting on some silly baby voice," she warned her aunt.

A few minutes later, Ellie found herself leaving their table and walking across the bar toward Rob Saunders, with Aunt Olive's last words still ringing in her ears:

"Make sure you sway your hips from side to side when you walk over to him... and give him a dazzling smile... don't be afraid to toss your hair... Giggle at anything he says and tilt your head to one side, so you can look up at him through your eyelashes... Remember, if you flatter his male ego and play him right, you should be able to get anything out of him."

Ellie walked slowly, trying to follow her aunt's instructions and sashay in a sexy manner. It was harder than she thought. Coordinating your hips to swing from side to side while still putting one foot in front of the other took some serious effort! She minced over to Rob but just as she reached his chair, she tripped and stumbled, lurching suddenly forward.

"Aaaagghh!"

Ellie would have fallen flat on her face if Rob hadn't jumped up and caught her. She fell neatly into his arms with an unladylike "OOMPH!" and felt him stagger slightly from the impact. Hastily, Ellie straightened herself, blushing furiously. Behind Rob's back, she saw Aunt Olive beaming and giving her a jubilant thumbs-up.

"Whoa! Are you OK?" asked Rob.

"Erm… yeah… sorry, I tripped," mumbled Ellie, hastily pulling her gaze back to him. She was mortified to discover that she'd left a smear of red lipstick on Rob's cheek.

"Oh! You've… erm… got some lipstick on your…" She pointed helplessly. "I'm so sorry—"

"Hey, no problem. You can leave lipstick on me anytime." Rob grinned. He picked up a napkin from the bar counter and wiped his face, then he looked her up and down, his eyes glowing with appreciation. "Say… you look kinda familiar. Have we met?"

"Yes, I was in your cocktail class."

Belatedly, Ellie added a giggle: "Hee! Hee! Hee! Hee!"

Rob looked startled by her high-pitched laughter. Then he snapped his fingers. "I remember! You're the pĩna colada girl!" He patted the empty bar stool next to him. "Can I buy you a drink?"

Ellie took a deep breath, gritted her teeth, and simpered at him. "Thank you!"

Chapter Fourteen

"So… do you come here often?" Rob Saunders asked.

Really? Ellie resisted the urge to roll her eyes at the clichéd chat-up line. *Remember what Aunt Olive said: giggle, smile, flatter his ego*, she reminded herself.

"Oh, I'm staying at the resort," she said, fluttering her lashes. "Hee! Hee! Hee! Hee!"

Rob gave her a funny look. "Uh… and you're here on vacation?"

"Uh-huh." Ellie batted her lashes for all she was worth. Rob was really gawking at her now. Ellie felt her confidence rising. *Maybe Aunt Olive's right. Maybe the red lipstick works. Maybe Rob is completely mesmerized by me now and under my spell—*

"Do you have something in your eye?" he asked in concern.

Ellie flushed. "No, no… I'm fine." She abandoned the eyelash fluttering and tried tilting her head to one side and giving him a coy look instead. "Erm… I really enjoyed your cocktail class."

"Thanks! That's great to hear. I hope I've convinced you to try some more cocktails now, other than piña coladas," he said, smirking.

Ellie gave a shrill giggle. "Oh, yes, you've totally opened my mind," she gushed. "I'll never look at cocktails the same way again! Hee! Hee! Hee! Hee!"

Rob eyed her warily and shifted slightly back on his stool. "So… uh… what'll you have?" He gestured to the bar menu and pulled out the insert which listed the cocktails. "How about a cocktail?"

Ellie tilted her head the other way and mustered up another coy look. "Oh, I never know what to choose. It's such a big menu, it's so confusing!" she said in her best impression of a helpless female.

Rob looked down at the cocktail menu in bewilderment. "It's eight drinks."

"Well… erm… eight is a big number," said Ellie with another shrill giggle. "I don't know… you choose for me!"

Rob turned to the barman and gave two cocktail orders, while Ellie wondered frantically how to turn the subject to his uncle.

"It's so nice to be with someone who knows how to order drinks," she cooed. "So… erm… how did you get into the cocktail thing?"

"I've always been interested in cocktails," said Rob. "I worked as a bartender while I was in college, and got into mixology pretty quickly. I had a natural talent with the shaker, you know?"

"Really?" Ellie squealed, opening her eyes very wide. She cocked her head to the side even more, then winced as she felt a spasm in her neck.

"Are you OK?" asked Rob, really beginning to eye her uneasily now.

"Uh... yeah... yeah, I'm fine," muttered Ellie, rotating her neck gingerly.

Oh sod this, she thought. *This is whole seduction thing is stupid! I'm just going to be myself.*

Straightening up again, she gave Rob a friendly smile and said in a normal voice: "You've got a great teaching style, you know—you make everything seem so normal and accessible. Your class really helped to break down the mystery surrounding cocktails for me. I think one reason I always ordered piña coladas was because they're safe and familiar. All those other cocktails seemed too fancy and I didn't feel sophisticated enough to order them. So I just stuck to what I knew."

"That's exactly it!" cried Rob, punching a fist in the air. "That's awesome to hear you say, because that's exactly what I've been trying to achieve. People are intimidated by the whole idea of cocktails, you know? They think mixology is complicated, but I want to demystify it, make it more accessible to everyone." He looked at her earnestly. "I've got big plans. I want to open a cocktail bar where people are encouraged to be really hands-on, like even mixing drinks themselves, maybe. Then they can learn more about what actually goes in their cocktails, the different rums used, the mixers and garnishes…"

"Wow, that sounds great," said Ellie with genuine interest. "I'd love to go to a place like that and I'm sure lots of people would too."

"Yes, that's what I told my uncle! I said it was a business idea with awesome potential, but he just wouldn't take me seriously." Rob made a sound of frustration. "He still treated me like a boy, and wouldn't even let me dip into my inheritance to help finance a start-up. The money was mine anyway! He had no right to—" Rob broke off suddenly. There was an awkward silence, which he tried to cover with a weak laugh. "Uh... yeah... well..."

"I'm sorry about your uncle," said Ellie. "It must have been a horrible shock."

Rob shook his head in disbelief. "You can say that again! I'd just been with him only an hour ago, you know? He was fine. And then—boom!—a few hours later, I get the news that he'd been found dead... and now they're saying it could be murder!"

"You say you saw him an hour earlier?"

"Yeah, I went to his room to speak to him again about my business proposal. I'd tried to talk to him earlier, but he wasn't in the mood to listen. So I took all my projections and business plans over to show him, plus the design schematics I'd got for the bar and the info about the site I'd found in downtown St. Pete. I thought if he saw all the stuff, he might finally take me seriously." Rob scowled. "No such luck. He wouldn't even look through the papers."

"And he seemed totally fine to you? He didn't seem sick or mentally affected in any way?"

Rob shrugged. "I guess he seemed a bit slower than normal and he was slurring his words slightly. He was pretty cranky, actually; kept saying he wanted to be left alone to sleep. But it was a hot afternoon, you know, and people get drowsy in weather like that. Plus, he'd been drinking—he had this huge Scorpion Bowl on the table in front of him. Man, that stuff has like three liquors in it, and a bowl is meant to be shared, not drunk by one person! So I wasn't really surprised."

"Weren't you worried about him, drinking all that by himself?" asked Ellie.

Rob shrugged again. "No, not really. Uncle Walt could hold his alcohol. Anyway, I've seen him drunk before. He usually just sleeps it off."

"So he was still conscious when you left him?"

"Oh yeah! He was sitting up and talking and stuff. Do you think I would have left him if he looked sick?" said Rob indignantly. "Anyway, Tonya was still in the suite with him when I left."

Ellie looked at him in surprise. "She was? But I thought... Tonya told the police that she left the suite while you were still with your uncle. Therefore *you* are the last person to have seen him alive."

"What?" cried Rob. "That's not true! Tonya was the last person who was with Uncle Walt. She was definitely still in the suite when I left—she took a call on her phone and I heard her talking out on the balcony. She was talking to some girlfriend, I think, asking what they were doing and stuff."

So had Tonya lied to the police? wondered Ellie. She thought back to the scene at the marina earlier that day, when she had boarded the *Saunders Spirit* by mistake: it was obvious Tonya hadn't been a loyal, loving wife. Ellie had also found a box of Valium in the cabinet, which meant that Tonya had had easy access to the drug which had killed her husband. And if she really was the last person left in the suite with him, she could have easily removed the ceramic bowl, which had contained the drink and the incriminating traces of diazepam.

But why would she dispose of it so close to the suite and in a random potted palm? thought Ellie, frowning. Surely Tonya would have tried to get rid of it farther away, so that it was less likely to be found and linked to Saunders's death? *Unless she did it on purpose,* thought Ellie grimly. Maybe she was trying to frame Sol for her husband's murder, so she wanted the Scorpion Bowl to be found wrapped in his apron...

"Uh... are you OK?"

Ellie blinked and came out of her thoughts with a start. She found Rob looking at her quizzically and realized that she had been staring into space for ages. *Great. Some seductress I'm turning out to be,* she thought. *First I scare him by laughing like a demented hyena, then I blank him completely!*

"Sorry!" She gave Rob a contrite smile. "I was just thinking... erm... how strange the whole thing is. I mean, who would want to kill your uncle?"

Rob shrugged. "Uncle Walt had a lot of business interests and he could be pretty ruthless. I guess you make enemies."

"So you don't agree with what the police think—that Sol, the head waiter at *Hammerheads Bar and Grill,* could be responsible?" asked Ellie.

"Well, it *is* kinda strange that the Scorpion Bowl was found wrapped up in his apron," Rob admitted. "And you *do* hear these stories of waitstaff getting vindictive. You know, like spitting in your soup and stuff."

"There's a big difference between spitting in your soup and murder!" said Ellie sharply. Then she took a deep breath and let it out slowly. It was bad enough that she wasn't flirting with Rob—she didn't have to bite his head off as well!

"Sorry," she said again with another apologetic smile. "I just think it's unfair to pin it on someone who might not have done it. A false murder conviction could ruin Sol's life."

Rob shrugged. "He's just some waiter anyway."

Ellie recoiled, staring at the young man in front of her in disgust. Until now, she had thought that Rob was a bit self-centered and immature, but decent enough overall. But now she realized that, in his own way, he was as much of a spoiled, callous "rich brat" as Tonya Saunders. He wasn't really that upset about his uncle's death—other than as an inconvenience to his own business ambitions—and he didn't care at all about anyone that he regarded as "staff."

"Actually, you know what? I don't think I'll be able to stay for that drink after all," she said coolly, sliding off her stool. "Thanks anyway. It was nice talking to you. Good luck with your bar."

"But…" Rob Saunders started to protest but Ellie ignored him and walked slowly back to her aunt's table.

Chapter Fifteen

To Ellie's surprise, when she got back to her own table, she found that her aunt wasn't alone. There was a middle-aged gentleman sitting next to Aunt Olive. The two of them were downing whiskey shots, and talking and laughing uproariously. Ellie's eyes widened as she saw her aunt slap the man playfully on his arm and flutter her eyelashes coquettishly. With Earl on the scene, she had thought her aunt would be reining in her romantic dalliances, but obviously Aunt Olive believed in keeping her options open.

Still... Ellie looked curiously at the middle-aged man. He wasn't the suave, good-looking type usually favored by Aunt Olive. Oh, he was smartly dressed in a suit and tie, but it was in a somber professional style, reminiscent of an accountant or lawyer. His chubby face was flushed and he was obviously immensely flattered by her aunt's flirtatious attentions. In fact, Ellie felt like she was intruding as she joined them at the table.

"Oh. Ellie..." Aunt Olive looked nonplussed for a moment when she saw her niece. "I thought you were having a drink with that nice young man?"

"I changed my mind," said Ellie shortly.

"Oh... well... you don't have to hang around because of me, poppet," said Aunt Olive with a meaningful look. "I'm sure you want to get back to the suite and freshen up, after our boat trip. Don't let me keep you!"

She wants me to go and leave them alone, Ellie realized in surprise. It was a strange role reversal—like a teenager who finds their parent wanting to stay out late or be left alone with their new crush. Giving Aunt Olive and the man an awkward nod, Ellie left the bar and walked out of the lobby. Slowly, she made her way back to the villa suite that she shared with her aunt.

Dusk was falling now and Ellie stopped for a moment by the pool deck, looking out past the pool to the beach beyond. She couldn't see the waves clearly anymore, but she could hear them faintly in the distance. The sound was soothing, as was the gentle chirping of insects coming from the greenery around her. Ellie took a deep breath and let it out, feeling some of the anger and indignation from her conversation with Rob Saunders drain from her.

Turning, she was about to continue down the path which led to her aunt's villa when she paused. *I'll go and see Blake*, Ellie thought with a sudden smile. She didn't want to admit it but she'd missed Blake that day. She'd been so looking forward to their date the night before and felt a bit bereft by the sudden cancellation.

Maybe Blake won't be feeling as tired as he expected, she thought. *Maybe we could still get a table at this fish shack place he was going to take me to or somewhere else... or we could just stay at the resort. An evening picnic out on the beach would be really romantic...*

Humming a happy tune to herself, Ellie retraced her steps partway and took a different route—the one which would lead to the long building housing many of the resort offices, including the resort clinic. Most of the windows were darkened now but she was hoping that Blake might still be in the clinic, finishing up some medical notes. She was just about to climb the steps to the clinic door when a resort buggy drove past. It slowed down next to her and the pleasant-faced young man in the typical resort uniform of polo-shirt-and-khakis combo called out to her:

"Are you looking for the doc, ma'am?"

"Yes," said Ellie.

"He just left for the evening," said the man. "I saw him lock up when I was passing a few minutes ago. Must have gone home."

"Oh," said Ellie, disappointed.

"Is it a medical emergency, ma'am?" he asked.

"Oh no, nothing like that. Blake—Dr. Thornton is… erm… a friend," Ellie stammered, blushing.

"Ah…" The man smirked and Ellie wondered what he had heard on the grapevine. She'd quickly learned, since arriving at the Sunset Palms, that gossip flourished at the resort. The staff loved to spy on and speculate about the guests, as well as talk about each other. She was sure that Blake, as the most eligible bachelor in the local community, attracted rampant speculation, and his frequent meetings with the new English girl hadn't gone unnoticed.

Now the young man's smirk widened as he said: "Well… since you're a personal friend of the doc's, you might like to stop by his condo."

"His condo?"

"Yeah, Dr. Thornton lives onsite. The resort has a small number of staff condos. They're that way…" He pointed down the pathway. "You follow this until you get to the end and go through a bamboo fence marked 'Private.' You'll see a walkway on the other side which winds around a small garden. The staff condos are on the other side. The doc's is the last one in the row, next to a big clump of dwarf palmettos."

Ellie thanked him and watched the buggy roll away again before following the man's directions. She had just stepped through the bamboo fence when she encountered a familiar sleek black figure.

"*MIAOW!*"

Ellie shook her head and chuckled as she looked down at Mojito the resort cat. "You! Is there anywhere in the resort that you don't get into?" She bent down to pat the cat. Mojito purred loudly, arching her back with pleasure. Then she turned and trotted ahead, leading the way as if she knew where Ellie was going.

"Oh no, you're not fooling me again," said Ellie as she followed the cat. "I'm going to avoid any condo you walk into!"

She found the row of staff condos fairly easily and walked alongside until she reached the end. Darkness had fallen now but the area was well lit with tall lamps spaced out at intervals next to the path, as well as the porch lights from each condo. There was a large clump of short, shrub-like palms next to the last condo, just like the guy in the buggy had said. Mojito rubbed herself against one of the palmetto trunks and Ellie paused absentmindedly to stroke the cat again. As she was straightening, however, she heard the sound of a door opening. She looked up to see two people coming out of the last condo, the light spilling out from the doorway clearly illuminating their features.

The first was a beautiful young black woman and the second was Blake. They were talking as they stepped out of the door and their voices carried clearly in the night air.

"...don't wait up for me tonight," the woman was saying as she stepped out of the door.

"You know I'm going to have a sleepless night if you're not back," said

Blake.

The young woman laughed. Ellie froze, her eyes widening in shock, as she saw the woman turn back to Blake and throw her arms around his neck, reaching up to whisper something in his ear. Ellie couldn't bear to watch anymore. She spun around and jerked sideways, out of sight behind the palmetto clump. She leaned against it, facing away from Blake's condo, and closed her eyes. The sharp edges of the palmetto fronds pricked the skin at the back of her neck, but she didn't move. Her breath came fast and ragged. *Did they see me? Oh God, I can't bear it if Blake saw me watching...*

She heard someone walking past and withdrew even farther around the side of the palmetto clump. The young woman went by, passing just a few feet away. She had her head down, busily texting on her phone, and barely glanced at the palmetto clump as she passed. Ellie watched her figure shrink into the distance, then she turned to peek through the palmetto fronds again.

Blake was still standing in the open condo doorway, staring after the young woman and frowning. Then he turned and looked directly at the clump of palmettos. Ellie's heart jumped into her throat. Had he seen her? The light from the porch and the nearby lamp didn't quite reach the clump, so most of it was in shadow. Still, Ellie shrank down even more amongst the palm fronds. She almost wished that she could burrow into the middle of the clump and disappear!

She heard footsteps approach and her heart began hammering. What was she going to say to Blake? How was she going to look him in the eye? She heard him come closer... and closer...

"Hello! What are you doing here?"

Ellie gasped and almost sprang up,

then she caught herself as she realized that Blake was still talking... but not to her. She could hear him murmuring and chuckling on the other side of the clump, and when she raised herself slightly from her crouched position and peered through the fronds, she saw that he was bending over and patting Mojito.

"*MIAOW!*" the cat said, rubbing herself against Blake's ankles.

Then, to Ellie's relief, Mojito trotted purposefully toward Blake's condo door. He hesitated a moment, then followed the cat. A minute later, they both went inside and the door shut quietly behind them. Ellie waited a moment, then released the breath she had been holding. Mojito had saved her from being discovered.

She stepped out from behind the palmetto clump. Her heart was thumping uncomfortably in her chest. In her mind's eye, she could see another doorway—this time back in London—

with a different man and woman stepping out. It had been the day she had finished work early and returned to the apartment she shared with her boyfriend, only to see him step outside with another woman. She had stood, frozen with shock and disbelief, and watched as the other woman kissed her boyfriend passionately on the mouth before sashaying away. Ellie could still remember the horrible mixture of betrayal and devastation. Now those feelings washed over her again.

No. No, it can't be happening to me again. There has to be an explanation, she told herself. *Blake isn't like that. He wouldn't do this to me.*

But it was hard to deny what her eyes had seen. True, she hadn't seen them kissing, but there had been a closeness between them that had been evident, even from a distance. From the young woman's words, she was obviously spending the nights at Blake's condo.

And judging from her ethnicity, she wasn't likely to be his sister!

Although she could be an adopted sister or a cousin, Ellie told herself desperately. *Or a friend who needs a couch to sleep on...*

But she knew that she was just clutching at straws. Nine times out of ten, the most obvious explanation *was* the real explanation.

Is this why Blake suddenly cancelled our date last night? wondered Ellie. *Was he with that young woman? He must have been! That's why he sounded so strange on the phone and why he put me off when I suggested waiting for him or meeting up later... He'd wanted me out of the way!*

But then why had Blake bothered to arrange the date in the first place? *It wasn't as if I made all the running,* Ellie thought. *Blake made it clear—or at least, he seemed to—that he was just as keen on me and wanted to see more of me.*

Or maybe I read too much into things? Ellie thought miserably. After all, it wasn't as if they had made an official commitment to each other. They had gone on a few dates together but there hadn't been any serious talk about their feelings for one another or a future together. Maybe in Blake's book, that meant he had every right to play the field as much as he wanted to.

How ironic, Ellie thought bitterly. *Here I was worrying about how to keep things light and breezy when Blake had never treated me as anything more than a casual fling all along!*

Feeling hurt and angry and a million other things, Ellie backed away until she was at a safe distance, then she turned and ran all the way back to her aunt's villa.

Chapter Sixteen

"It just isn't the same here without Sol, is it?" said Aunt Olive, looking around the restaurant with a sigh as they entered the next morning.

They had both woken up late that morning and had decided on a more leisurely brunch at *Hammerheads Bar and Grill* again, rather than rushing to make the busy breakfast buffet before it closed. Aunt Olive headed for her favorite table on the outdoor terrace and Ellie silently followed. She agreed with her aunt that the restaurant felt strangely bereft without Sol's smiling presence. Mr. Papadopoulos had revealed that the county sheriff's office had originally refused bail but, after some negotiation, he had managed to get them to agree to release Sol from custody, on the condition that the head waiter remained at the resort while the investigation was ongoing.

Ellie wondered where Sol was staying and how he was coping. "I'm going to try and see Sol after breakfast," she said.

She felt a stab of guilt again as she thought of Sol. She knew it was silly but she couldn't help feeling that if she hadn't identified the apron as his, the police wouldn't have jumped on Sol so quickly as the chief suspect in the case. She sighed as she sat down next to her aunt and picked up the menu listlessly. When her order finally came, Aunt Olive stared at it in astonishment.

"What's the matter with you, dear?" she asked

"Nothing. Why?"

Aunt Olive indicated Ellie's plate, which held a small portion of fruit salad and nothing else. "Usually your plate is piled high with bacon and pancakes and all sorts of things. How come you're eating so little today?"

"I'm not very hungry."

Aunt Olive made a tutting sound. "You're not going on some ridiculous diet, are you? Don't tell me you suddenly think you look fat."

"Well, I *have* put on quite a few pounds since I came to Florida," said Ellie.

"Oh fiddle-faddle! You need curves to fill out a bikini properly. I never thought you'd be one of those girls who's neurotic about her figure." She gave Ellie a sly look. "Is this because of your young man?"

"He's not my young man," snapped Ellie.

"Ooh... Have you had a lover's tiff?"

Ellie flushed. "We haven't had an 'anything'! This is nothing to do with Blake!"

Aunt Olive raised her eyebrows, her skepticism clear. "It's not like you to be so out of sorts, poppet. If it's not Blake, then what is it? Are you upset because I didn't come back for dinner last night? I'm sorry—I probably should have rung or sent you a message. I just forgot the time. Anyway, I thought you'd probably just call room service and have a cozy evening in, if you weren't meeting Blake."

"No, of course I'm not upset that you were out last night—you know that, Aunt Olive," said Ellie quickly. In truth, she had been grateful that her aunt had been out all evening and hadn't returned until late. It had meant that she hadn't had to face any awkward questions about her obvious distress when she had returned to the villa yesterday evening.

And by the time her aunt had come back, close to midnight, Ellie had had a good excuse to hide in her bedroom with her lights off, thus avoiding any conversation.

Now, though, she mustered up a smile for her aunt and said, "I certainly don't expect us to have dinner together every night. I did exactly what you said—I ordered room service and had a cozy evening in, curled up in front of the TV. It was lovely and relaxing," she lied. "Anyway, what about you? You seemed to be having a fantastic time with that gentleman at the lobby bar. Who is he? Did you spend the whole evening with him?"

Aunt Olive's eyes gleamed. "His name is Norman Hill. He's a lawyer and the executor of Walter Saunders's estate. And he told me some *very* interesting things over dinner last night..." She waggled her eyebrows meaningfully.

"What sort of things?"

"Apparently it's well known that Tonya only married Walter Saunders for his money. And what's more, Saunders seemed to be well aware of that fact too—so much so that he had a specific prenuptial agreement drawn up before their wedding."

"A prenup agreement?"

"Yes. Listen to this: it states that if Saunders catches Tonya being unfaithful to him in any way, she would be cut off without a cent."

"Really?" said Ellie, thinking of the sordid scene she had stumbled on yesterday on the *Saunders Spirit*. "That really changes everything."

Aunt Olive nodded. "Oh yes! According to Norman, Saunders's current will shows Tonya inheriting almost all of his personal wealth— everything that isn't tied up in Rob's trust fund. But it's dependent on that prenup condition being met. If Saunders dies without ever publicly accusing Tonya of infidelity, there is no challenge to the will and she inherits everything!"

"So if Tonya was worried that Saunders was about to find out about her affair, she could have decided to cut her losses and kill him first—before he had the chance to make it official," said Ellie.

"Exactly," said Aunt Olive. "How's that for a perfect motive?"

"Wow." Ellie looked at her aunt admiringly. "How did you manage to get all this information out of Saunders's lawyer?"

Aunt Olive gave a coy smile. "I told you, there's nothing like a well-deployed eyelash flutter and show of cleavage. *Even* when you're sixty-four."

Ellie started to answer but she was interrupted by the sound of a cellphone ringing. It was a popular iPhone ringtone and it was incredibly loud. Aunt Olive started groping in her handbag for her phone, as did several other guests at nearby tables. But one person after another picked up their phone, only to find that it wasn't ringing, and looked around in bewilderment.

Ellie turned her head, trying to trace the sound. She realized that it was coming from above and, when she looked up, she gave an exasperated laugh. A familiar scarlet macaw was perched on the frond of a palm tree that was leaning over the restaurant terrace. Hemingway was swaying from side to side as he whistled the ringtone tune:

"Toodoo-da-doo-da-doo-doooo..."

The sounds coming from the parrot's beak were so realistic, Ellie wasn't surprised that so many people had been fooled. Now the other guests looked up as well, pointing and laughing as they realized that they'd been bamboozled by the mischievous bird.

"You know, I read an article once that birds can even mimic the sound of microwaves and chainsaws," commented Aunt Olive.

"Oh no, don't give Hemingway any more ideas!" said Ellie.

They spent the rest of breakfast steadfastly trying to ignore the multiple "fake" iPhones that kept ringing from the trees above them, and they could see the guests at the other tables doing the same.

"At this rate, nobody is going to be picking up their phone when it really rings later today," said Ellie with a chuckle as they finally rose from their table.

"Well, I'm going to ignore mine for the next few hours anyway," Aunt Olive declared. "I'm going to find a nice comfy hammock and really dig into this book." She pulled a large hardback out of her beach tote.

"What's that?" asked Ellie, eyeing the heavy tome. "That hardly looks like beach reading!"

Her aunt laughed. "No, it's not, but I think it's going to be fascinating all the same. It's a book written by psychologists about social learning theory and I think it'll give me some great ideas for writing characters."

"What's social learning theory?"

"It's basically the idea that people learn by watching others. And this is especially true of kids: they are constantly watching their parents, seeing how they solve problems, learning their moral codes."

"Moral codes?"

"Well, for example, if a child hears his mother lie to the cashier at a restaurant and say that he's only eleven—even though he's actually twelve—just so she can get a discount at the buffet, he'll grow up thinking it's OK to lie in that kind of situation. And he will mimic that behavior when he gets older."

"I suppose that makes sense—although it didn't really work with me," said Ellie with a laugh. "Despite Mum and Dad's best efforts, I haven't grown up anything like them at all! I don't think like them, I don't behave like them, I don't value the same things they do..."

"Ah, that's because you're a throwback like me," said Aunt Olive with a wink. "You hark back to the early adventurers and explorers in our family tree. Which is just as well, since we need a bit of spirit and recklessness in this generation to offset all that saintly responsibility and relentless organization shown by your sister!"

Ellie giggled. Her elder sister Karen was the model wife, mother, career woman, and community volunteer, who had every minute of every day planned out to perfection and always seemed to know where she was going in life and how to get there. Ellie had always felt a combination of envy and resentment toward her sister for her perfectly managed life.

Still, it's a much more boring life, she told herself. Karen would never have come to Florida on the spur of the moment and she certainly wouldn't have gotten herself involved in a murder investigation!

Chapter Seventeen

Ellie had expected Sol to be placed in one of the "staff condos" at the resort, so she was surprised when she asked at reception and was told that he was in one of the guest rooms on the upper levels of the main resort building. Maybe the police had thought this would keep Sol closer to the lobby and the central resort offices, therefore making it easier to keep him "under surveillance." The room was one of the budget options, facing onto the road running past the resort rather than facing out toward the beach, but it was still a very comfortable accommodation. Ellie was touched by

Mr. Papadopoulos's compassion and generosity toward his employees.

She paused outside the door and was just lifting her hand to knock when she heard raised voices coming from inside. Looking down, she saw that the door was slightly ajar and she was surprised to hear Sol's normally calm tones sounding harsh and impatient:

"...you shouldn't be here, Jasmine!"

"I was worried about you, Dad! The police wouldn't tell me anything and—"

"*You've been talking to the police?* I told you to stay away from them! You know what's at stake and if they find out what happened that night—"

"I'm not stupid, OK? I know how to talk to them. Anyway, Carson's not interested in me. He's, like, only focused on the murder case."

There was a heavy sigh. "Jasmine, I can't be worrying about you too, on top of everything else right now."

"You don't have to worry about me, Dad! I told you, I'm not stupid. Jeez, I'm not a kid anymore, OK? I know what I'm doing." There was a pause, then Jasmine's voice lost some of its bravado and she added in a more subdued tone: "It's not just you. I wanted to talk to Ava too. She hasn't been returning any texts or calls, so I've been trying to find her. I thought she'd be at *Hammerheads* or something."

"I thought Mr. Papadopoulos gave her time off for as long as she needed?"

"Yeah, she took a day off yesterday but she's back at work today. She was like: 'I don't wanna stay home alone.'"

"How is she?"

"She's messed up, Dad. She's really scared."

"Well, tell her there's nothing to worry about. I won't say anything to the police—"

"But... Dad! What if they think it's

you?"

"Don't worry, honey—they can't convict me without proof. Right now, it's all circumstantial. I just need to stick to my story and we'll be fine."

"But Dad, the cocktail bowl was found wrapped in *your* apron! That's, like, the murder weapon, 'cos he was poisoned, right? That's not just circumstantial! And I was talking to some of the other staff at *Hammerheads*: they said Detective Carson was there yesterday, questioning them and trying to, like, make a case against you. He really thinks that you're guilty and he's just looking for a way to pin the murder on you—"

"It'll be fine, honey. You've just got to trust me, OK?"

There was a cry of frustration, then the sound of footsteps hurrying toward the door. Before Ellie could step away, the door to the room was flung open and she found herself face to face with the woman she had seen leaving Blake's condo the night before.

Ellie stared, speechless, as a tumult of emotions washed over her. Jasmine was even more beautiful up close, with large, thickly fringed eyes, a generous mouth, and luminous skin the color of dark caramel. She had inherited her father's tall, rangy figure—which translated into the kind of slender hips and long limbs that graced catwalks and fashion magazine covers. Her dark brown hair was styled in a mane of ringlets which framed her face, making her eyes look even larger and more luminous. Looking at her, Ellie felt suddenly short, plain, and dumpy.

"Who are you?" Jasmine asked, looking at Ellie quizzically.

Ellie suddenly realized that her right hand was still half-raised, as if to knock on the door. Hastily, she dropped it to her side, flushing. "I… erm…"

"Ellie!" Sol had come to the door as well and was now standing beside Jasmine. He looked surprised but pleased to see her.

"I... I just came to see how you are, Sol," said Ellie, backing away from the door. "But I don't want to disturb you. I'll come back another time—"

"I'm going anyway," said Jasmine abruptly.

Without a word to Ellie, she stepped out of the room and stalked away down the corridor. Sol watched his daughter disappear around the corner with troubled eyes. Then his face brightened as he turned back to Ellie and said:

"That's real nice of you to come and see me, Ellie. Especially since... well, a lot of people wouldn't be eager to associate with a suspected murderer."

"Oh, that's bollocks!" said Ellie. "I know you're not a murderer!"

Sol gave her a heartfelt smile.

"Thanks for your faith in me." He beckoned her into the room. "Come in."

"Are you allowed visitors?" asked Ellie.

Sol shrugged. "Beats me. Everything's been so unclear. First they said they were going to keep me in custody and that they wouldn't let me out on bail." He gave an ironic laugh. "Not that I could get hold of the kind of money needed anyway! Then Mr. Papadopoulos did a deal with his county sheriff friend and they agreed to let me out, under Mr. P's personal guarantee, provided that I stay at the resort." He glanced up and down the corridor. "I thought I'd have a police guard or something..."

"Maybe there's been new evidence and they don't consider you such a strong suspect anymore," said Ellie hopefully.

"Well, until someone tells me

otherwise, I'm going to treat this like a social visit," said Sol with an emphatic nod. He led Ellie into the room, shut the door firmly behind them, and gestured to a chair beside the bed.

Bending to look in the mini-fridge, he said: "I'm afraid I can't offer you a glass of fresh OJ or your other favorite drinks at *Hammerheads*, but there's bottled apple juice, if you like, or Coke or Sprite?"

"Actually, I think I'd prefer a cup of tea," said Ellie.

"Tea? Now?"

Ellie laughed. "You obviously don't know us English well enough. Yes, tea—anytime. Especially when you're feeling a bit down or tired or upset, there's nothing like a nice, hot cup of tea to bolster the spirits and make you feel better."

"Well, oh-kay..." said Sol, shaking his head skeptically. But he set about making a mug of tea.

Ellie watched him surreptitiously, noting that in spite of his attempt at cheery conversation, Sol seemed to be under a lot of strain. He was normally such an upbeat person—his beaming face and warm personality were some of the things that made *Hammerheads Bar and Grill* such a welcoming place. But now, Sol's wide smile and twinkling eyes had been replaced by a downturned mouth and eyes that were bloodshot and crinkled with worry. He might have been putting on a brave face for his daughter, but Ellie had a feeling that Sol wasn't so confident about the police releasing him.

"Erm... so how have you been?" Ellie asked as she took the mug from him and wrapped her hands around its comforting warmth.

"Oh... not too bad," said Sol lightly as he sat down on the edge of the bed with a can of Coke for himself.

"Have the police made any progress with the case?" Ellie asked.

Sol shook his head in frustration. "I don't know. They won't tell me anything. They just keep asking me the same questions over and over again."

Ellie took a deep breath and said: "Sol, I know we don't know each other that well and I'm not really a close friend or family... but... but I hope you *do* see me as a friend."

Sol looked surprised and deeply touched. "Well, now... thank you, Ellie. I can't tell you how much I appreciate hearing that. And yes, I do see you as a friend," he added. "I know you've only been in Florida a few weeks but I don't think it's always about how long you've known someone. Sometimes, you just click with a person, right?"

"Yes!" said Ellie, giving him a warm smile. "Yes, that's exactly how I feel, Sol." She hesitated, then added: "And as your friend, I really want to help you. I… erm… I couldn't help overhearing some of your conversation with Jasmine just before I came in. I don't mean to pry, but what you said about Ava—"

"What about her?" asked Sol quickly.

"You're covering up for her, aren't you?" asked Ellie bluntly.

Sol flinched. "I don't know what you're talking about."

"I heard you and Jasmine talking. You said Ava didn't need to worry because you weren't going to say anything to the police. And yesterday morning, when Detective Carson came to question you at *Hammerheads*, you nearly said that you gave your apron to someone. It was Ava, wasn't it? Why did you change what you were going to say? Was it because you didn't want to get Ava in trouble? Please, Sol…" Ellie looked at him earnestly. "I can help you! But I need to know the truth. You're covering up for

Ava, aren't you? You *did* give her your apron that night."

Sol looked torn for a moment, then finally he sighed and said, "Yes. I lent Ava my apron after she spilled some soup on hers. I had to leave the restaurant early that evening, so I knew I wouldn't be needing it. I took it off and gave it to her just before I left."

"And she never gave it back to you?"

Sol hesitated. "No. I never saw it again—until the next morning when Detective Carson showed it to me in the evidence bag."

"So that means Ava was lying!"

"Not necessarily," said Sol quickly. "She could have taken the apron off and left it in the kitchen before she left the restaurant."

"Then how did it end up wrapped around the tiki bowl and dumped in the potted palm?"

"I wish I knew."

Ellie frowned. "It doesn't make sense. If one of the other suspects was trying to frame you—for example, Tonya Saunders—how would she have got hold of the apron?"

"She could have sneaked into the *Hammerheads* kitchen, I guess—"

"And just conveniently know where Ava left your apron?" said Ellie sarcastically. "And how did she sneak in, in the first place? It's not that easy— someone would have noticed and asked her what she was doing there. Same for Rob Saunders. And I'm not even going to bother with Roy Mack since he'd left the resort by then. So none of these other suspects could have easily got hold of your apron. Besides, why would they bother? It seems like a lot of work just to frame you. Rob doesn't even know you. As for Tonya, couldn't she have got her revenge another way?" Ellie shook her head decisively. "No, the much simpler explanation is that *Ava* had the apron. She wouldn't have had to sneak into the kitchen—in fact, she was already wearing it! Which also means that chances are, Ava is the one who wrapped the apron around the tiki bowl and dumped it in the potted palm."

Ellie glanced at Sol. She could see from his expression that he had already followed this train of thought himself and come to the same conclusion.

"Sol... why are you covering up for Ava?" she asked.

Sol passed a hand over his eyes and sighed. "Look, Ava has had it pretty tough in life and I don't want to make things any harder for her. I don't know what really happened that night, but I know she had nothing to do with Walter Saunders's death."

"She was the one who found the body though," Ellie pointed out. "And it's looking like she was the one who removed the empty Scorpion Bowl from the crime scene and tried to hide it."

Sol shook his head obstinately. "Ava's a good kid. I *know* she's not a murderer."

Ellie looked at Sol in some surprise. The way he spoke about the waitress sounded more personal than just as a senior work colleague. "You sound like you know Ava well?"

"I should. She's been Jasmine's best friend since elementary school. Watched the two of them grow up together. Ava's like a second daughter to me," said Sol with a small smile. "In fact, I was the one who got her the job at *Hammerheads*. Jasmine had just got a part-time job over at a diner in the marina, and Ava was feeling kind of left out. So I talked to Mr. Papadopoulos and he agreed to give her a try. The resort wouldn't normally hire someone so young and with so little experience, but Ava's a smart kid and I knew she would learn fast. I promised Mr. P that I'd keep an eye on her and that she wouldn't let him down."

Sol heaved a sigh of frustration. "Until what happened with the Saunders, Ava hadn't put a foot wrong. She had a great manner, all the guests liked her, and she was quick, efficient, and smart. She was a great waitress."

"Well, have you told the police all of this?" asked Ellie. "If you explain everything, I'm sure Detective Carson will understand and be reasonable."

"I'm not so sure about that. That man is looking for a scapegoat and if it's not me, then it'll be Ava." Sol looked at Ellie pleadingly. "And you can't say anything to the police either! You gotta promise me!"

"But..." Ellie began to share some of Jasmine's previous frustration with her father. "You can't just take the blame for everything, Sol! You could end up convicted for a murder you didn't commit!"

"I'll be OK," said Sol with a wan smile. "Don't worry about me. I've got broad shoulders."

Chapter Eighteen

Ellie left Sol a short while later and took the elevator back down to the first floor. She walked slowly through the large spacious lobby, with its pretty beach-themed décor and potted palms scattered between the comfortable couches in the seating area. Normally, she would have been eagerly people-watching and speculating about the new guest arrivals, but today she was too preoccupied with her own thoughts to even notice the people she passed.

Her recent conversation with Sol had left her feeling even more frustrated about the case. Ellie was sure that Ava was somehow involved in Walter Saunders's murder. When she had crashed into Ava that night, she had assumed that the girl was rushing out of Saunders's suite in a panic to get help. But now she wondered if, in fact, the girl had actually been rushing out to *get rid of evidence*.

Ellie paused and closed her eyes briefly, straining her memory and trying to conjure up in her mind's eye the scene that night. Had Ava been carrying a bundle when Ellie had crashed into her? It had been dark and everything had been in such a confusion... No matter how hard she tried, Ellie just couldn't recall a clear picture. All she could remember was walking along and then suddenly being knocked to the ground by another body colliding into hers. By the time she had picked herself up and recognized the other person as Ava, she had been too distracted by the waitress's breathless exclamations to pay any attention to what the girl was wearing or carrying.

But she could easily have been carrying the ceramic bowl, wrapped in the apron, thought Ellie. *It might have been knocked to the ground after our collision. So Ava let me go into Saunders's suite first while she used that time to retrieve the bundle and hide it in a nearby potted palm.*

That would explain why it hadn't been hidden farther away, Ellie realized. It had been something that puzzled her because it had seemed illogical for someone to go to the trouble of removing the evidence, only to stash it in a hiding place just outside the building! Surely the murderer would have made the effort to dispose of it farther away from the crime scene? If it had been Rob Saunders, he could have easily dropped it somewhere en route on the beach. Similarly, Tonya could have taken it to the *Saunders Spirit* and dropped it over the side into the water. And even if Roy Mack had been around to remove the ceramic bowl, wouldn't he have taken it off site to get rid of it? None of those suspects would have just hidden the bowl in a potted palm right outside the building.

But if Ava had removed the empty cocktail bowl, then it all made sense. She had probably planned to get rid of it farther away, but when she happened to collide with Ellie, she was forced to change her plan. She pretended that she had actually been rushing to get help and then used the time when Ellie went into the suite to retrieve the bundle and shove it into a nearby pot. Maybe she had planned to return later to remove the bundle, but with the police arriving and searching the area, Ava had been forced to abandon that idea.

Ellie remembered the way the girl had jumped when the officer brought the bundle to Detective Carson. At the time, she'd simply thought that Ava was still traumatized by finding the body. But now she realized that it was more likely that the young waitress had had an unpleasant shock when she saw the bundle in the police officer's hands.

Ellie sighed with frustration again. Ava could have been the murderer! Why was Sol protecting the girl? She stepped through the rear lobby doors and was just starting down the wide walkway leading to the beach, when she spied a familiar young black woman leaning against a pillar nearby. It was Jasmine. She was smoking and staring off into the distance, but when she glanced around and saw Ellie, she started guiltily. Hastily, she dropped the cigarette, grinding it out with one heel.

"You're not gonna tell my dad, are you?" she blurted. "He doesn't like me smoking."

Ellie shook her head, surprised by

Jasmine's almost child-like worry about her father's reaction. She would have expected that at eighteen, Jasmine was more likely to be defiant about smoking, rather than being anxious about "getting in trouble." She stared at the young woman in front of her. In spite of her age and sophisticated appearance, Jasmine seemed quite immature.

"So you're Ellie, huh?" said Jasmine, looking her up and down. A little smile hovered at the corners of her lips. "Blake's been telling me a lot about you."

Ellie stiffened and felt a mixture of hurt and anger flood through her. It was bad enough that Blake was seeing another woman behind her back, without gossiping about her too! Did they laugh about her together? Make fun of her being a total sucker for his charms? She gave Jasmine a curt nod and turned away.

"Wait!" Jasmine took a step toward

her and said: "Uh... I wanted to apologize..."

Ellie paused and looked back at her in surprise.

"I... I was kinda rude back there, in my dad's room," muttered Jasmine. "I should've said goodbye to you or something when I was leaving. I was just so mad at Dad..."

To Ellie's surprise, she saw tears start to the other girl's eyes. Jasmine dashed them away angrily and sniffed, trying to get her emotions under control. She seemed suddenly very young and vulnerable, and in spite of herself, Ellie felt a stab of sympathy and compassion for the other girl.

"I'm sorry about your father," she said awkwardly. "I'd really like to help."

"Dad always wants to take on everything himself!" Jasmine burst out. "He's always, like, doing stuff to protect others, even if it means taking the blame himself."

"Like with your friend Ava?" asked Ellie. "Your father is covering up for her, isn't he?"

Jasmine looked away. "I... I don't know."

"Jasmine, did Ava tell you what really happened on the night of the murder?"

The other girl shook her head. "Ava doesn't tell me stuff anymore. Ever since she started seeing her new guy, she's been different."

"Ava got a new boyfriend? When?" asked Ellie, wondering if it had a bearing on the case.

Jasmine shrugged. "I dunno. Like... a month ago? She was acting all weird and then one day I asked her about it and she told me she's seeing this new guy." Jasmine wrinkled her nose. "He's, like, so much older than her!"

Ellie had to bite her lip to stop herself

saying something about pots and black kettles. She was surprised at Jasmine's reaction given that Blake was in his early thirties, and Jasmine was only eighteen herself. Surely her own involvement with a much older man would have made her more sympathetic to or open-minded about her best friend's new romance? Or was this one of those cases where people just didn't apply the same judgments to themselves?

Jasmine sighed. "We used to, like, do everything together, you know? When me and Ava met at school, we were BFFs instantly! I never had a mother growing up and Ava was the same. Even her father was out of the picture, so Dad sort of took over. She was always over at our place or I was over at hers. We liked my place better though, 'cos her grandma was so strict, whereas Dad... well, I could always sorta twist him around my finger," said Jasmine with a laugh. Then she sobered. "But it's all different now.

Ever since Ava met her new guy, she's always standing me up to go and spend time with him instead. Or she's working here at the resort. I've hardly seen her in the last few weeks!"

"Jasmine, do you think Ava could have anything to do with the murder?" Ellie asked.

The other girl shifted uneasily. "No! No, I'm sure Ava would never hurt anyone," she said. "Besides, it's dumb to think that she would murder this Walter Saunders guy just because he was rude to her. I mean, come *on!* You get stuff like that happening all the time. Rich folk acting rude and stuck-up… that's, like, the usual deal when you're waitressing. I get it down at the diner too. You just ignore them."

"Well, maybe this time, Ava just lost her temper," suggested Ellie. "I mean, everyone has a limit, don't they? And I was there, I saw it all happen—the Saunderses really were unreasonable.

Maybe Ava got fed-up."

"No, not Ava," said Jasmine, shaking her head. "Ava's, like, super-focused when she wants something and she was doing real good here at the resort. She was even talking about getting an apprenticeship or a diploma in hospitality. She was like: 'Just because I didn't get a college scholarship like you doesn't mean I can't make something of myself'—so I'm sure she's not gonna let some stupid rich guy with a big mouth ruin her future, by doing something crazy just to get even with him!"

Ellie walked away a few minutes later, mulling over what Jasmine had told her. She still didn't believe that Ava wasn't somehow involved in the murder. Something just didn't add up about the girl's story from that night. Besides, Ava was the most logical person to have been in possession of the apron wrapped around the empty Scorpion Bowl... and didn't they say that the most logical explanation was usually the most likely one too?

But at the same time, Jasmine's description of her best friend had been quite persuasive. It did seem like a silly motive for a murder, especially when Ava had so much to lose. It was true that waitstaff must have to deal with dozens of rude, arrogant customers every day. Ava sounded like a girl who was clever and ambitious—would she really throw away her future and commit murder, just for a petty chance at revenge?

Chapter Nineteen

Ellie was quiet and thoughtful during lunch with her aunt. They'd opted to eat out of the resort for a change and had gone to dine at a quaint local café famous for its eclectic menu and its raspberry iced tea. The food had been excellent, with Ellie trying everything from the Mediterranean eggplant and Low Country shrimp to their signature grouper encrusted in crunchy pecan crumble. She polished it all off with a delicious coconut layer cake, smothered by a fluffy layer of coconut frosting, and had two tall glasses of the famous iced tea.

"Well, I'm glad to see that your appetite seems to have returned. It's important to keep romantic disappointments in perspective, you know," commented Aunt Olive as she eyed Ellie's empty plate. She held up a hand as Ellie started to protest. "No, don't tell me there's nothing going on between you and Blake. I know a lover's tiff when I see one. But I'm not going to pry," she said virtuously. Then she instantly contradicted herself by leaning toward Ellie and adding: "Is it the sex? Or another woman? If he's just a bit slow in the bedroom department, I can give you a few tips—"

"*Aunt Olive!*" gasped Ellie, shocked and exasperated.

"What?" said Aunt Olive airily. "Oh, don't tell me you're embarrassed. Really, I never thought the younger generation would be so prudish. After all, sex is a perfectly normal thing between two consenting adults. But of course, when you're still getting to know each other, things don't always come naturally. You have to figure out how to tell him what you like. But don't worry, poppet—men can be trained, just like puppies. In fact, I could tell you some stories about the time I was seeing that lovely chap in the navy—"

"Uh... that's OK, Aunt Olive... I... erm... I don't need any tips or advice in that area right now," said Ellie hastily. She tried to change the subject. "You know you've been talking about taking me to do some sightseeing? How about this afternoon? We could go and visit that alligator farm that Earl told us about."

Aunt Olive wrinkled her nose. "Alligators?"

"Yes, they're a famous Florida attraction, aren't they?"

"Well, I don't know about 'famous attraction.' I've always just thought of alligators as part of the landscape here," said Aunt Olive.

"Yes, but it will be fascinating to learn all about how they are farmed and what they eat and how they reproduce and all that!"

"I suppose so." Aunt Olive looked slightly bewildered by Ellie's sudden enthusiasm. "I didn't realize you were so interested in alligators, poppet."

"Well, it's not just an academic interest," Ellie admitted. "The farm Earl mentioned is owned by Roy Mack, who was Saunders's business partner. He was the one who ordered the Scorpion Bowls in the first place, and I *did* see him put something into Saunders's cocktail."

"But I thought you said they were just dried scorpions—you saw them yourself. And you said that Mack put the same thing in his own drink."

"I know, I know," said Ellie, putting her hands up in a defensive gesture. "I know what you're going to say: Mack is the *obvious* suspect, so chances are he's not the killer—"

"Well, that's not always true," said Aunt Olive. "Generally it holds, but you could have a case of double bluff. I've done it in my own books. Still, it does seem very unlikely. If Mack wanted to poison Saunders, you would have thought that he would have found a more discreet way to do it, rather than tamper with the drink that he orders for Saunders himself—and in a public restaurant, no less!"

"Yeah, you're right," Ellie admitted. "Still, I'd like to go and check the farm out. After all, Saunders *was* planning to go there the next day—maybe there is a connection."

It wasn't the whole reason, although Ellie didn't want to admit to her aunt that the other reason was that she just wanted to stay away from the resort for a bit longer. She'd slept very badly the night before and she was desperately trying not to think about Blake and the scene she had witnessed. So focusing on the mystery of Walter Saunders's murder provided a welcome distraction. Besides, Blake had also tried to call her twice since last night and had sent her several text messages. She was ignoring them all, but she had a feeling that he might start going around the resort looking for her next. She just didn't feel able to face him at the moment. She knew staying out was just a cowardly attempt to delay the inevitable—she would have to face Blake at some point—but right now, she still felt too wounded to want to deal with things.

Half an hour later, a taxi dropped them off in front of a large gate designed in the hacienda style, with red roof tiles and stucco siding. A fiberglass model of an enormous alligator with its jaws wide open stood beside the entrance arch, together with a sign bearing the words: "GROOVY GATOR FARM." They joined the line of tourist groups and families waiting to get tickets, and a few minutes later strolled into the large property.

Ellie was surprised to see that it looked more like a small zoo than a farm. She went ahead, eagerly peering into cages and enclosures, and getting a general feel for the place. In addition to alligators, the farm also kept a few native reptiles and amphibians, including skinks and anoles, gopher tortoises, rattlesnakes, and an impressive six-foot-long specimen of the fearsome cottonmouth snake. All the animals looked alert and healthy, and their enclosures were clean and well-designed.

"This looks like a very well-run place," commented Aunt Olive, coming up to join Ellie next to the cottonmouth enclosure. "Nothing suspicious so far."

"Yes," Ellie agreed. She was feeling a bit disappointed. Somehow, her overactive imagination had conjured up a stereotypical villain's lair, with dirty, graffiti-sprayed buildings and shifty-eyed men slinking around. But the reality was nothing like that. The alligator farm was a bright and cheerful tourist attraction that seemed to be doing a very comfortable business.

Am I barking up the wrong tree? Ellie wondered. She thought back to the conversation she had overheard between Walter Saunders and Roy Mack. Maybe she had read too much into things. Just because Saunders had wanted to check the accounts didn't have to mean anything illegal *was* actually going on. Plus, Mack hadn't seemed remotely perturbed by the prospect of his partner arriving the next day to do a personal audit. In fact, she even recalled him offering to give Saunders a tour.

"Oh look!" said Aunt Olive, pointing to a group of people nearby, congregating around a young man.

He was blond, with boyish good looks, and—from the logo on his khaki shirt—Ellie guessed that he was one of the alligator farm staff. He was announcing a guided tour around the farm and people were eagerly lining up.

"Let's join the tour," said Aunt Olive suddenly.

"I thought you said you hated tours," said Ellie. "You were just telling me, back at the resort, that you don't like having to follow someone around, listening to them talk. You said you'd rather walk at your own pace and read the signs yourself."

"Yes, but a woman's entitled to change her mind, isn't she? Especially when the tour guide looks like that," said Aunt Olive with an impish smile.

"Aunt Olive!" said Ellie with mock horror. "He's young enough to be your grandson! Really, first that lawyer guy and now this... what about Earl?"

"What about him?"

"Well, I thought you and Earl were—"

"Earl and I are just good friends," said Aunt Olive loftily. "I can be friends with lots of men, can't I? In fact, the more handsome they are, the more friendly I feel!" she added, tossing her head back and laughing heartily.

Ellie shook her head with a mixture of exasperation and amusement as she followed her aunt over to the group. Somehow, Aunt Olive always seemed to make her feel like an old prude—which was ridiculous, considering that she was the younger person there!

They joined the other tourists and filed obediently after the tour guide as he began leading the way around the farm. The first tank he stopped at held an unusual resident: an alligator with ivory-white skin and pinkish eyes. Ellie stared at it in fascination and blurted out:

"Is it real?"

The tour guide laughed next to her. "Oh yes, very real! This is Mr. Ice, our albino alligator. He's not a Florida native, actually—he's originally from the Louisiana bayou. And he's one of the rarest alligators in the world."

"Yeah, there are only, like, about a hundred albino gators, right?" a man called out from the group.

"Yes, that's right," said the tour guide. "Now, does anyone know why Mr. Ice's skin is white?" He looked at the children in the group, but the man spoke up again.

"It's the gene thing—you know, a mutation. Stops your skin producing this stuff called melanin. Same thing we have in our skin. It's what gives us a tan."

"Yes, that's right, sir." The tour guide smiled politely, then turned to the kids again. "Does anyone know why it's bad not to have melanin?"

Before any child could answer, the man piped up again:

"Makes 'em easy to see, doesn't it? Albinos can't camouflage so they can't hunt. Plus they're easy prey when they're babies. Oh, and it makes them real sensitive to the sun too. Like, sunburn, you know? Which is tough 'cos gators need to bake in the sun to warm up. They're cold-blooded so they can't move around until they warm up enough. Kinda like charging a battery, you know?" The man chuckled, heedless of the fact that the other people in the group were starting to give him irate looks.

"Uh... yes, that's right. You're very knowledgeable, sir," said the tour guide, his polite smile starting to look strained now. He turned back to the rest of the group. "And one more thing you may not know: myth says that if you look into the eyes of an albino alligator, it will bring you good luck. So make sure you get a good eye-to-eye with Mr. Ice!" He turned away. "Now, if you'll follow me, I'll show you some more of our toothy residents…"

The group moved on to a larger but shallower pool, surrounded by a low fence. Ellie saw several small reptiles swimming in the water and basking at the edges of the pool. *They're baby alligators*, she realized in surprise. They were only about the size of a large lizard and she couldn't quite believe that these would one day grow up into the big, scary predators she had seen on TV and in YouTube videos.

"Why aren't their mommies with them?" one of the children asked.

"Well, we're taking care of them now," the tour guide explained. "But in the wild, alligator mommies do stay with their babies, sometimes up to two years. That's pretty unusual in the reptile world."

A familiar man in a baseball cap and fanny-pack pushed himself to the front of the group and chimed in eagerly: "Yeah! Did you know that alligator mothers stand guard over their nests? When they hear the babies hatching outta their shells, they even carry them into the water in their mouths."

Aunt Olive groaned and muttered, "Not him again. Why is there always one know-it-all in every group, who loves the sound of his own voice?"

Ellie laughed. She could see, though, that several others seemed to share her aunt's sentiments and were throwing the man dirty looks. He seemed remarkably thick-skinned, though, and oblivious to how obnoxiously he was behaving. He was now busily telling everyone who would listen the difference between an alligator and a crocodile.

"It's all here, see?" he said, pointing to his own nose. "It's the shape. Gator snouts look like a U; crocs look like a V."

"Yes, and you can also tell because alligators have an overbite so when they shut their jaws, you can only see the top row of their teeth. In crocodiles, you can see both top and bottom teeth protruding," said the tour guide, trying to wrestle his position of authority back from the man. "Crocodiles are also bigger. The males can get as big as twenty feet, whereas gators usually only get up to around fourteen feet max. And of course, the other big difference is that gators prefer to live in freshwater." He smiled at the children and beckoned to them. "Now, if you'll come with me, I'll show you some of the babies' Mamas and Papas."

They followed the tour guide to a large lagoon at the rear of the park. One side of the lagoon was spanned by a raised wooden boardwalk with high wooden railings. The tour guide led them onto the boardwalk, pausing when he reached the halfway point. Ellie leaned over the railing and saw what looked like dozens of gnarled logs floating below. Then she caught sight of a pair of eyes protruding above one of the "logs" and realized that they were all alligators. She marveled at how still they could be, floating motionless in the water. Several of the other visitors were looking over the railing too, including the annoying "know-it-all" guy, who was leaning out precariously far and waving his baseball cap tauntingly in front of the nearest alligator.

"I wouldn't do that if I were you," said the tour guide.

"Oh, it can't see me anyway," the man scoffed. "Gators have crap eyesight."

"That's a myth," said the tour guide bluntly. "They actually have pretty good eyesight; in fact, they've got 360-degree wide-angle vision because they have eyes on the sides of the head. And don't believe the myth that they can't move fast on land either," he added, giving the man a pointed look. "They might not be able to run for miles, but they can put on an impressive burst of speed, which is definitely faster than your reflexes."

Before the man could answer, the tour guide turned pointedly away from him and said to the rest of the group:

"And that concludes our official tour, but if you want to hang around, we're going to be doing the last feeding of the day before the park closes. So you're welcome to stay here and watch the alligators have their dinner!"

Ellie started to join the other tourists at the railing, but Aunt Olive didn't follow. Instead, she headed off the wooden boardwalk and sank onto a bench near the walkway leading back to the farm entrance. Stretching out one foot, she wriggled her ankle and grimaced.

"My feet are killing me," she

complained. "I'm going back to the entrance. I think I saw a small café there. I've seen alligators being fed before anyway, so I'm not fussed if I miss it. But you stay, poppet, and enjoy the show."

Chapter Twenty

Ellie waited until her aunt had hobbled out of sight before rejoining the group on the wooden walkway. The tour guide had left them and now reappeared on a wooden platform on the other side of the lagoon. He was wearing a headpiece with a microphone and carried a large bucket. Ellie noticed that several of the alligators in the pool seemed to be stirring. They were gliding through the water toward the platform, their tails waving from side to side. Soon, the area of water right beneath the platform was churning with alligator bodies trying to climb on top of each other.

"Well, as you can see, these guys are hungry!" said the tour guide with a laugh.

He reached into the bucket and pulled out a rat by its tail. It was obviously dead, but still, Ellie couldn't repress a shudder as she watched him dangle the limp rodent over the hungry reptiles below. Several alligators jumped and lunged, missing the rat by a few inches. The guide dangled the rat temptingly above several snouts before finally releasing it into the jaws of one particularly large alligator. Ellie heard its jaws shut with an audible *SNAP* which drew gasps of appreciation from the watching crowd.

The tour guide repeated the performance several more times, to the delight of the visitors, especially the kids. Ellie, however, quickly lost interest and, after watching for a few moments, turned away. When she tried to get off the boardwalk, however, she discovered that her way was barred by the rest of the group. Rather than push through them, she turned in the opposite direction.

Maybe I can get off the boardwalk at the other end, she thought, drifting away from the group. *Once I get off it, I'm sure I can circle back to that bench Aunt Olive was sitting on and retrace my steps to the entrance...*

She followed the narrow boardwalk as it sloped down toward the other bank of the lagoon and curved around some dense vegetation, blocking the tour group behind her from sight. Just when she thought the boardwalk was going to join a public walkway, she found that it ended abruptly at a tall gate which was part of the brushwood fence encircling the lagoon enclosure. There was a large sign marked "PRIVATE – NO ENTRY" secured to the gate.

Curious, Ellie leaned forward and pressed her eye to a gap between the panels of the fence. She could see an open area beyond, surrounded by several low buildings and enclosures. It didn't have the pretty greenery and landscaping that surrounded the areas at the front of the farm. Instead, a lot of the space was concrete and functional. She could see hose pipes, brooms, and a wheelbarrow filled with a collection of loose debris, feces, and uneaten food. Obviously, this was the "backstage" area of the farm, where the more mundane, practical aspects of breeding and farming alligators were carried out.

Ellie was just about to retreat when she spied two men stepping out from one of the buildings and walking toward her. She felt a spurt of excitement as she saw that one of them was Roy Mack. Their words drifted faintly over as they approached but Ellie could only catch snatches of their conversation.

"...everything ready?" Roy Mack was saying to the other man.

"Yeah, boss... good numbers... best haul so far..."

"Good... keep an eye on things..."

"...thought the fallout from Saunders's murder was gonna ruin everything—"

Roy Mack made an impatient noise. "You just keep your mind on your own job... told you to leave Saunders to me."

"...lucky break for us he got himself murdered," said the other man, grinning.

"Nothing to joke about... Saunders and I go a long way back—"

"You sound like you're gonna miss him, boss!"

"...credit where it's due... it wasn't for him, there'd be no farm and you'd have no job," said Roy Mack bluntly.

It was frustrating not being able to hear properly. Ellie pressed harder against the gate, straining her ears to catch every sound. The next moment, she gasped as the gate swung open suddenly and she pitched forward with a cry. She tumbled through and landed in a heap, right in front of the two men.

"What the heck!" Roy Mack stared down at her. He frowned but, before he could say anything, the other man stepped forward and caught Ellie's arm roughly, pulling her to her feet.

"What are you doing here?" he snapped. "This area is off-limits to visitors."

"Sorry. I thought there was another way off the boardwalk in this direction—"

"Can't you read the sign?" demanded the man, pointing at the open gate where the words "PRIVATE – NO ENTRY" were prominently displayed.

"Look, I said I'm sorry," said Ellie. "And if you really want to keep visitors out, shouldn't you have locked the gate?"

"We did! It should be locked—unless you messed with it?" He gave Ellie a suspicious look.

"I didn't 'mess with it,'" said Ellie indignantly. "I just leaned on the gate slightly and it swung open. Maybe one of your keepers forgot to lock it." She rubbed her arm and added, "There's no need to be so aggressive about it! Why are you so worried about me coming through? Have you got something to hide?"

The man took a menacing step toward Ellie. "What're you suggesting—"

"Hey, man! This is cool!"

They were interrupted by a familiar voice and Ellie turned to see Mr. Know-It-All coming up the boardwalk. He stepped through the open gate and joined them. "Is this the backstage tour? Huh?" he asked, grinning. "Count me in! I've done a ton of reading on gators, you know. I'll bet I know as much as you do.

Test me—go on, test me!"

Ellie wanted to burst out laughing when she saw the expression on the face of the aggressive man in front of her. Suddenly, she felt a lot more charitable toward Mr. Know-It-All.

Roy Mack stepped forward, putting a restraining hand on the other man, and assumed a pleasant expression.

"I'm sorry, sir… ma'am… this is a restricted area." He looked at Ellie, giving her an apologetic smile. "You'll have to excuse my farm manager Sam. He takes the issue of safety at the farm very seriously, especially visitor safety, so he may have… uh… overreacted. This is a working area, you see, with heavy equipment and access to our breeding enclosures. We don't want anyone having an accident or wandering into the wrong place and putting themselves in danger."

"Oh. Well, as I said, I'm sorry—I didn't

mean to trespass," said Ellie, feeling slightly embarrassed now in the face of Roy Mack's polite apology and reasonable explanation.

"Hey, did you say there are more gators back here?" asked Mr. Know-It-All, looking eagerly around. "Can we take a look?"

To Ellie's surprise, Roy Mack hesitated for a moment, then said, "Well, this area is normally off limits to the public, but it's nice to see visitors so interested in our gators. Since there are just the two of you, I guess we could give you a small tour. Sam, why don't you show our two guests around?"

The farm manager started to protest but, at a look from his boss, he fell into a sullen silence.

Roy Mack turned back to Ellie and Mr. Know-It-All. "Just make sure you follow Sam and don't touch anything or enter any area unless he tells you to, OK?"

"Okey-dokey!" said Mr. Know-It-All, gleefully following the farm manager as the latter turned and stomped off.

Chapter Twenty-One

Ellie trailed behind the two men. She wasn't actually that interested in seeing any more of the alligator farm—especially in the company of the surly Sam!—but given the goodwill gesture that Roy Mack was making, she felt like it would be rude to refuse. *Besides, this is a golden chance to snoop around a bit*, she told herself. Still, as she followed the two men around the various buildings, barns, and enclosures, she saw nothing suspicious. Just like the "public" parts of the farm, everything was clean and well-maintained, and looked like nothing more than a busy, prosperous farming facility and tourist attraction.

Sam showed them where the growing juveniles and sub-adults were kept, as well as the places where the alligators' food was prepared.

"So they don't just eat rats?" asked Ellie.

"Nah. That's just for the show. Most of the time, they get 'gator pellets.'"

"That's a specially formulated, high-protein diet which is enriched so that they get all the nutrients they need, right?" said Mr. Know-It-All.

Sam gave him a sour look, but didn't answer. Instead, he said, "We give 'em 'whole animals' too sometimes."

"What kind of 'whole animal'?" asked Ellie uneasily.

Sam shrugged. "Fish, chicken carcasses, rats and mice, chunks of beef, lamb, or pork... Gators will eat anything. They'll even take insects and vegetables and fruit."

"Wow," said Ellie, impressed. "I didn't think farmed alligators would be so pampered."

"You think we mistreat 'em?" asked Sam aggressively.

"No, no, that's not what I meant," said Ellie, thinking: *Bloody hell! This man is touchy!* "I just thought... well, I thought that pets usually get that kind of special treatment but not farm animals, livestock, you know..."

"There's actually very good research which shows that healthy animals grow better and produce much better yields, in any kind of farming," Mr. Know-It-All piped up. "So it's in the farmer's interests to keep his animals content and healthy." He turned to Sam. "Say! What do you do if a gator *does* get sick? It's not like you can take 'em to the vet, right?" He chortled.

"The vet comes to us," said Sam, unsmiling. "We've got a guy on call."

"Yeah, but a gator's not gonna let you examine it, like a dog or a cat, right? Is that when you tie them up? I've seen it on YouTube—you tape up the jaws, huh?" Mr. Know-It-All made a circular motion with one finger around his mouth.

"Yeah, we tie 'em up sometimes," said Sam. "But it stresses the animals out. Plus there's more chance of getting injured. So sometimes, we sedate 'em with drugs instead. Diazepam works great—"

"*Diazepam!*" cried Ellie.

Sam looked at her sharply. "Yeah. What's the problem?"

"N-nothing... I was just surprised that you can use the same thing you find in Valium on alligators," said Ellie, recovering quickly.

Sam shrugged. "Works the same way. Makes 'em nice and relaxed, easier to handle." He glanced impatiently at his watch, then said: "OK, show's over. I got stuff to do."

Ellie obediently followed the farm manager as he led them back to the gate connecting to the boardwalk. The wooden walkway was empty now; the feeding show was obviously over and the group had probably been escorted to the gift shop. Sam stood with his arms crossed and watched them until they had crossed the entire boardwalk and were safely on the other shore. Ellie could still feel his suspicious gaze trained on her as she started down the path which would take her back to the farm entrance.

"That was awesome, huh?" said Mr. Know-It-All, walking beside her. "I'm going to tell everyone I got VIP access to the back of a gator farm!"

"Mmm..." murmured Ellie absently.

Her mind was busy on other things— in particular, on what the farm manager had said about sedatives. Was it a coincidence that the very drug used in Walter Saunders's lethal cocktail should be the same drug used to sedate the alligators? It would mean that Roy Mack had an easily accessible supply of diazepam, if he had wanted to poison his business partner.

She came out of her thoughts to see that she had arrived at the farm entrance. There was a small gift shop next to the main gate, with an even smaller café attached, and she found Aunt Olive sitting at one of the outside tables.

"My goodness, poppet, you look like you're trying to solve all the world's problems at once! I didn't realize alligator-feeding would be so thought-provoking," teased Aunt Olive as Ellie joined her.

"I've been doing a lot more than just watching alligators eat rats," said Ellie, and she began to recount everything that had happened since they parted.

"Ooh, very interesting," said Aunt Olive, her eyes sparkling. "The plot thickens, as they say!"

Ellie sighed. "I'm so confused now. Before we came here this afternoon, I was sure that Ava was involved, but now I'm wondering if Roy Mack is as innocent as I thought. I mean, he *did* have an opportunity to poison Saunders's cocktail too. And from what I overheard just now, he does sound suspicious."

"Does he, though?" asked Aunt Olive. "All the things you heard—like the talk about 'keeping an eye on things'—could have an innocent explanation too. Those words could mean very different things in different contexts."

"Even the line about the fallout from Saunders's murder ruining everything?" said Ellie skeptically.

"Yes, even that. It could just be referring to the negative PR for the farm or the inconvenience of the police investigating them. Not because they're guilty but just because it's all an extra hassle."

"What about when Roy Mack said: '*You just keep your mind on your own job... told you to leave Saunders to me*'?"

"What about it?" said Aunt Olive. "He could have meant: leave him to deal with Saunders, in terms of soothing his business partner's anxieties. Not necessarily in terms of murdering him!"

"But his farm manager said it was a lucky break for them that Saunders was murdered," argued Ellie.

"Oh no, what you said you heard was the farm manager saying it was lucky that 'Saunders *got himself* murdered.' That's a subtle but important difference, poppet. If they had been involved in the murder themselves, wouldn't he have said it was lucky that 'we got rid of Saunders' or something to that effect?"

"Well, he could have been saying it in an ironic way," said Ellie. But she had to admit that her aunt had a point. "Maybe you're right," she conceded. "In fact, now that I think about it, Roy Mack actually told Sam off—he said that Saunders's death was nothing to joke about and that he had to give credit to Saunders for getting the farm off the ground. He actually sounded a bit sorry and upset that his business partner was dead."

"Yes, and I just saw something which could explain all that talk about being ready and 'good numbers'…" Aunt Olive nodded at the wall across from them.

Ellie followed her aunt's gaze and saw a poster stuck to the wall, advertising a charity fundraiser in downtown St. Pete. It looked like the gator farm was sponsoring the event. In fact, Roy Mack himself was headlining it, putting on a variety show of stand-up comedy, magic tricks, acrobatic stunts, and animal displays. The poster showed a picture of the farm owner wearing the traditional magician's top hat paired with the traditional khaki "alligator hunter uniform"; he was clutching a baby alligator in one arm while simultaneously doing card tricks with the other.

"Looks like Mack still likes to keep his hand in," Aunt Olive observed. "It's true what they say: once a showman, always a showman! Still, it's all going to a good cause," she added, noting the logo for the children's charity in the corner of the poster. "It's clever of him to combine his past career with his present one in a philanthropic way. Builds great goodwill for the farm and gives them great PR in the local community."

Ellie wasn't so interested in the event. Instead, she was feeling slightly deflated. "So everything I overheard could be innocent?"

Aunt Olive grinned. "Well, not every

bit of sleuthing turns up worthwhile leads," she said. "Otherwise my books would only be two chapters long!" She stood up briskly. "Come along, poppet. Let's go back to the resort. I think it's almost five o'clock and I am dying for a decent cuppa. *Not* one of those tall iced drinks that the Americans persist in calling 'tea' but a proper hot cup of tea brewed in a real teapot!"

Chapter Twenty-Two

Ellie was dismayed when they arrived back at the resort to see Blake in the lobby. He was standing at the reception counter, talking to Mr. Anderson the resort manager, but he broke off as soon as he saw her enter and came toward her.

"I'll just leave you two to your *tête-a-tête*," said Aunt Olive smoothly.

Ellie felt a flash of panic. She wanted to grab her aunt's arm and tell her not to go, but it was too late. Aunt Olive had already slipped away and was now trotting rapidly toward the rear lobby doors which led into the main resort grounds. Ellie took a deep breath and turned around to face Blake as he came up to her.

"Ellie! Are you all right? I've been trying to reach you—I called and sent you several texts, but you never replied. Is everything OK?" said Blake, his brown eyes warm with concern.

"Yes, of course. Why wouldn't it be?" asked Ellie coolly.

Blake stopped short. "Oh. I thought… It's just that I haven't seen you the last two days and—"

"Well, we don't live in each other's pockets, do we? You're obviously happy to suit yourself so I don't see why I shouldn't do the same."

"I… *what?*" Blake looked at her quizzically. "I'm sorry, Ellie—am I missing something here? You seem to be mad at me."

Ellie bit her lip to stop the torrent of

words that threatened to spill out. *Play it cool, be an ice queen*, she told herself. She was not going to humiliate herself by showing how upset she was over Blake's betrayal. She had gone through that once before already. Her cheeks still burned at the memory of her fight with her ex-boyfriend back in London, when she had discovered that he was cheating on her. She couldn't bear the thought of laying herself open like that again. So she raised her chin and fixed Blake with a cold look.

"No, I'm just mad at myself for being so stupid as to trust you. But I'm not going to make that mistake again." She turned to go.

"Now… wait a minute!" Blake said, starting to sound angry himself. He caught hold of Ellie's arm to stop her leaving. "You can't just freeze me out like that! If I've done something to make you mad, you've got to explain and give me a chance to apologize—"

"I don't need to explain myself. If anyone needs to do some explaining, it's you!" said Ellie, rapidly forgetting that she had intended to play it cool. "But I'm sure you'd just give me a load of lame excuses. The fact that you even have the nerve to ask me to explain shows what a totally unfeeling tosser you are, Blake Thornton!"

Blake shook his head. "I have no idea what you're talking about, Ellie."

His calm insistence pushed her over the edge. "I'm talking about seeing Jasmine coming out of your condo last night and kissing you!" she snapped.

Blake took a step back, a guarded expression coming over his face. "You were watching us?"

"I wasn't spying on you, if that's what you're implying," said Ellie tartly. "I went to find you at your clinic and you weren't there. Then one of the resort staff directed me to your condo. I just wanted to say hello and see if we could salvage our date from the night before… and when I got close, I saw you and Jasmine coming out of the front door. She was telling you not to wait up for her, and you were saying…" Ellie's voice wobbled. "…you were saying that you'd have a sleepless night if she wasn't there…"

Blake took a deep breath and let it out slowly. "Ellie, it's not what it looked like—"

"Then what was it supposed to look like?" demanded Ellie. "I saw the two of you with my own eyes, Blake! You were kissing—"

"That's definitely not true!" said Blake firmly. "You can't have seen us kissing because it didn't happen! Are you sure it was me that you saw with Jasmine?"

"Of course it was you! I'm not an idiot—I could see you both clearly. Jasmine started to walk away from you, then she turned and went back to you. I saw her throw her arms around you and reach up to kiss you—"

"No, she wasn't kissing me," Blake cut in quickly. "She was whispering something in my ear."

"Oh really? What? Sweet nothings?" said Ellie sarcastically.

Blake heaved a sigh of frustration. "Ellie, you can't jump to conclusions like this."

"Well, fine! If it's all so innocent, then tell me everything. Tell me why Jasmine was sleeping at your condo. Why was she with you? What did she whisper in your ear?"

"I... I can't tell you," said Blake. "But it's not what you think," he added hurriedly. "I promise you, there's nothing going on between Jasmine and me."

"If there's nothing, then why can't you tell me?" Ellie demanded.

"Look, I want to tell you but... I made a promise and I can't break my word, OK?" said Blake, looking agonized. "I need you to trust me, Ellie. I'm not seeing another woman behind your back. What you saw with Jasmine... there's a perfectly innocent explanation. I just can't give it to you right now."

Ellie stared into Blake's earnest face. She felt herself wavering and, for a moment, she almost softened. Then the memory of the fight with her ex-boyfriend came flooding back. He'd used the exact same words and phrases: *"It's not what you think... I need you to trust me, Ellie..."* Oh yes, she had trusted him. She had let herself be sweet-talked back into blind complacency, until she had walked into the bedroom, a few weeks later, and found her ex-boyfriend and the other woman in her bed.

I'm not going to be that fool again, Ellie told herself, straightening her back.

"Ellie...?" Blake took a step toward

her.

She backed away from him, shaking her head. "No... *No!*"

Whirling, she ran out of the lobby.

Chapter Twenty-Three

As she burst out of the rear doors, Ellie collided with someone who caught her arms to steady her.

"Ellie! My dear, where are you going in such a hurry?"

Ellie caught her breath and looked up to see the kindly, moustachioed face of Mr. Papadopoulos hovering above her.

The resort owner regarded her with avuncular concern, taking in her flushed cheeks and flashing eyes. "Are you all right, my dear? You look a little—"

"I'm... I'm fine," said Ellie breathlessly, trying to pull herself together. She forced a smile to her face. "Sorry to crash into you."

"Oh no, I was hoping to run into you— although perhaps not so literally," said Mr. Papadopoulos, chuckling. He took her arm and led her into a secluded corner of the small garden next to them, so that they could talk in privacy.

"I wanted to tell you some good news: it seems that the police might be revising their opinions about Sol's involvement with Walter Saunders's murder," he said. "There's still the issue of his apron being found wrapped around the empty cocktail bowl, of course, but as far as *opportunity*… They've double-checked the statements from Paolo, the bartender at the Tiki Bar, as well as the other staff in the *Hammerheads* kitchen, and it seems that Sol was never alone with the Scorpion Bowl before it was served to Saunders. Several of the other restaurant staff were near the bar and would have seen if he tried to tamper with the drinks. Therefore, it's unlikely that he had an opportunity to—unless you count Tonya Saunders's story of him deliberately tripping and spilling tainted tomato juice into the Scorpion Bowl." Mr. Papadopoulos waved a hand. "But even Detective Carson doesn't take such a far-fetched suggestion seriously. Far more likely for someone else to have tampered with the drink than for Sol to use such an elaborate ploy to poison Saunders's cocktail."

"So, according to the police, who *did* have a chance to tamper with the drink?" asked Ellie.

"Well, obviously the one with the easiest opportunity is Paolo, the bartender who made up the cocktail at the Tiki Bar. But there's no connection between him and the victim, plus he was surrounded by several witnesses who watched him make it and testified that he didn't add anything other than the basic ingredients. Therefore, the police aren't really considering Paolo a suspect. As for the others... there's the waitress Ava, who served the Scorpion Bowl to Saunders; there's Saunders's business partner Roy Mack, who was drinking with him at first; there's his wife, who joined him later and who carried the cocktail up to their suite; and lastly his nephew, who went to see him after Saunders returned to his suite. And who, according to Tonya Saunders, is the last person to see him alive—"

"That's not what Rob says," said Ellie quickly. "I spoke to him yesterday and he claims that Tonya was still in the room when he left. He heard her answering her phone. So he says *she* is the last person to have seen Saunders alive."

Mr. Papadopoulos raised his eyebrows. "They seem to be contradicting each other's stories. Did Rob Saunders definitely see Tonya in the suite?"

"No, apparently she was out on the balcony. But he definitely heard her talking on her cellphone and I don't think he's lying," Ellie said. She thought of the passionate scene she had stumbled upon on the *Saunders Spirit*, plus what Aunt Olive had discovered about the infidelity clause in the Saunderses' prenup agreement, and she added, "I think the police should question Tonya Saunders again."

"Well, she certainly had the opportunity to poison her husband, but does she have a motive?" said Mr. Papadopoulos. "At the moment, the majority of Saunders's estate goes to his nephew anyway. If she was really after the money, wouldn't it have made more sense for her to kill Rob?"

"I suppose so," Ellie admitted.

"I would have thought it's more in Tonya's interest to keep Walter

Saunders alive for as long as possible, because then she would have more chances to get him to alter his will and allocate a bigger share of his fortune to her. Plus, he was a generous man, so the longer he was around, the more wealth and assets she would have gained in the form of jewellery and other gifts."

Ellie thought back to the scene she'd observed at *Hammerheads*, when Tonya had been wheedling her husband to buy a new pair of pearl earrings, and again had to admit that Mr. Papadopoulos was probably right. Then she brightened as she remembered something.

"But Walter Saunders's generosity was conditional on the clause in their prenup agreement," she said.

Mr. Papadopoulos furrowed his brow. "What clause?"

"The infidelity clause, which said that if Saunders discovered that his wife was cheating on him, she would be cut off without a cent."

"My dear, how do you know this?" said Mr. Papadopoulos, looking at her in surprise.

"Oh... erm... Aunt Olive told me. She's... erm... great at ferreting out information like this. It's what makes her a bestselling mystery author," Ellie said glibly. "Anyway, the point is: if Tonya was having an affair and she was worried that Saunders might suspect, she would've had a very good reason to kill him before he confronted her. Because then she could maintain that she didn't break the clause and is entitled to her share of the fortune, as stipulated in his current will."

"Hmm... that would certainly be a strong motive. Well, I'm speaking to the county sheriff this evening so I will mention all this to him," said Mr. Papadopoulos. "Frankly, my dear, I think the police are a bit stumped by this case. If you have any other suggestions or insights, I'd be happy to pass them along." He looked at her inquiringly.

Ellie hesitated. She thought of Ava. Now was the time to share her suspicions about the young waitress. But something held her back.

"Have the police questioned Ava again?" she asked tentatively.

"The waitress? I'm not sure. I believe they took a statement from her initially, but they haven't spoken to her since." Mr. Papadopoulos smiled. "I actually asked them to go easy on Ava. She's only eighteen and I imagine that this whole episode has been very traumatic for her, especially given what happened with her parents."

Ellie looked at him quizzically. "What d'you mean? What happened with her parents?"

Mr. Papadopoulos made a tutting noise. "Oh dear, didn't you know? Well, I suppose you wouldn't, given that you're not a local. It was in all the papers at the time anyway, so it's in the public record and I'm not breaking any privacy laws telling you... Poor Ava: her mother tried to poison her father and was caught and arrested."

"Her mother *poisoned* her father?"

"Oh, you could say that it was justified—or at least provoked," said Mr. Papadopoulos quickly. "Ava's mother had been the victim of domestic violence for years. Her father routinely beat her mother and she was a regular visitor to the local ER. It was a tragic case. In the end, the poor woman obviously decided that she'd had enough. She had been prescribed some Valium for anxiety and she dissolved some in her husband's glass of whiskey."

"*What?*" gasped Ellie, staring. "*Valium?*"

"Yes, the same drug used on Walter Saunders, funnily enough. Luckily in

Ava's father's case, they managed to get him to the hospital before he went into cardiac arrest. He survived, which is just as well, otherwise her mother's conviction would probably have been more severe. As it was, she was given a light sentence in consideration of her mental state and other factors."

"What happened to Ava?" asked Ellie, horrified.

"Well, her father disappeared shortly afterwards, so she was sent to live with her grandmother. This was over ten years ago now, so she was only seven or so at the time, but certainly old enough to understand what was going on." Mr. Papadopoulos sighed. "Poor child. It must have been hard enough to be effectively 'orphaned' all of a sudden, without all the media attention that surrounded her as well. It was a great scandal at the time. It's been a while now and many people have forgotten the case, but when Sol brought Ava to meet me, I immediately remembered her. We don't normally employ anyone as young as eighteen, you see, but I made an exception in her case. I really wanted to help her and give her the chance to thrive. I was even thinking of offering her an apprenticeship..." He sighed again. "From what I heard, she was doing really well until this Saunders incident blew up. Hopefully they will find the killer soon and Ava will be able to get on with her life."

Ellie didn't answer. She was thinking uneasily: *But what if Ava* is *the killer?*

Chapter Twenty-Four

The sun was slipping down the horizon by the time Ellie left Mr. Papadopoulos and continued her way through the resort grounds to her aunt's villa. She paused when she reached the pool, looking beyond the neat rows of lounge chairs to the view of the beach in the distance. There was a spectacular sunset visible through the silhouettes of the palm trees and Ellie could see how Sunset Palms Beach Resort must have gotten its name. She would normally have been spellbound by the view, but this evening she found it difficult to focus on the beauty around her.

Instead, Ellie was thinking about the conversation she had just had with Mr. Papadopoulos and she was feeling guilty. She should have shared her suspicions about Ava with the resort owner. It was her duty to report anything which might have a bearing on the investigation. But at the same time, she felt terrible at the thought of snitching on the young waitress. Especially now that she knew the girl's tragic backstory.

Although that very backstory could add to the case against her, thought Ellie uneasily. She recalled what Aunt Olive had said about social learning theory and how kids modelled their parents' behaviours, including their moral codes. If, as a young impressionable child, Ava had seen her mother use poison to solve a problem—would she be tempted to use the same method too? Was it just a coincidence that the drug used to poison Walter Saunders was the very same one that Ava's mother had used?

Ellie sighed, unsure what to do with her dilemma. Then she had an idea: *I'll go and speak to Ava myself first*, she decided. *At least then I've given the girl a chance to give her side of the story. Then I can decide whether to go back to Mr. Papadopoulos tomorrow morning and tell him everything.*

Ellie retraced her steps around the pool deck until she arrived at the entrance of *Hammerheads Bar and Grill*. The restaurant served food all day, but right now it was relatively empty; it was that quiet time when many guests had returned to their rooms after a busy day's activities and were washing or changing and getting ready to go out for the evening. In another hour, the dining room and outdoor terrace would probably be buzzing with people, but right now, none of the tables were occupied.

Ellie was pleased to see a young

woman in waitstaff uniform walking around, lighting candles on the tables. It was Ava. Ellie hadn't seen the girl since the night they discovered Saunders's body. Now, as she approached the young waitress, she noted that Ava seemed to have aged five years since then. There were dark circles under her eyes and lines of strain around her mouth.

"Ava?"

The girl jumped and whirled around, nearly dropping the candle she was holding.

"Y-yes?" she stammered, fumbling to right the candle.

"Sorry, I didn't mean to startle you..." Ellie offered a friendly smile, which the other girl didn't return.

Instead, Ava eyed her warily and said, "Can I help you, ma'am?"

Ellie hesitated, wondering how to broach the subject. "I... erm... I was just wondering how you are? I mean, it was a nasty shock, finding a dead body like that. I hadn't seen you around so I wondered if you were OK."

"The resort gave me some time off," Ava said. "But I'm back now."

"Oh. Well... I hope you haven't found the whole thing too traumatic?"

Ava shook her head but didn't answer. *Bloody hell, she's hard work!* thought Ellie. She bit her lip and tried again.

"Have the police been coming back and asking you loads of questions?" she said in a chatty tone, leaning close and trying to create an intimate "girlie buddies" atmosphere.

"N-no... they only questioned me once, on the night we found the body," said Ava.

"Oh, lucky you! The police keep coming back to ask me more stuff," Ellie lied, pouting in an exaggerated manner. "Especially about that apron. They're obsessed with it!"

Ava paled slightly. "Th-the apron?"

"Yeah, you know, the apron that was wrapped around the empty Scorpion Bowl they found just outside the building. The police are trying to work out who hid the bundle in the potted palm. I'm really worried that they're focusing on Sol because it's his apron. He could end up facing a homicide charge!"

Ava looked aghast. "But Sol said... he said they wouldn't really... Do you really think the police would charge him with murder?"

"Well, they think the person who hid that cocktail bowl is probably the murderer, and since Sol's apron was around the bowl... Of course, it could have been someone else who took his apron. In fact, I'm sure that's what happened." Ellie gave a theatrical sigh. "I really hope the police find the real person who hid that bundle, because I just don't believe that Sol could be the murderer and I don't want him to be wrongly convicted." Ellie looked Ava straight in the eye. "I mean, Sol is such a nice guy, such a decent man. Wouldn't it be awful if he ended up taking the blame for something he didn't do?"

Ava nodded and looked miserable.

Ellie snapped her fingers, pretending to suddenly think of something. "Hey, I just remembered, Sol mentioned that he lent *you* his apron that night after you spilled some soup on yours—"

"Yes, but I took it off and left it here in the restaurant, when I finished my shift," said Ava quickly. "I told the police that already."

"But then that means someone must have sneaked into the restaurant and nicked the apron?" said Ellie, making a great show of furrowing her forehead. "Doesn't that seem a bit strange to you?"

Ava shrugged. "People do weird things."

"Who d'you think might have done it?" asked Ellie chattily. "Do you think it could have been Saunders's wife? She was such a nasty cow, wasn't she? Or do you think another guest at the resort could have done it? Although I don't know what motive they'd have for wanting to kill Saunders... Besides, don't you think it's a bit elaborate for them to go to all the trouble of sneaking into the restaurant to steal an apron, just to wrap the bowl in? Couldn't they have used something else? It would make much more sense if the person who removed the bowl was someone who worked here at the restaurant. What d'you think?"

"I... I don't know," said Ava, shifting uneasily. She looked desperately around, as if searching for a way to escape the conversation. "Look, I... uh...

I need to get going... I gotta, like, prepare the tables for the dinner rush..."

"Oh, of course. Sorry, I didn't mean to hold you up from your work," Ellie said breezily. "Well, I'm sure there are people out there who know more than they're letting on—I just hope they will come forward and tell the police the truth before it's too late. You know, I've read some awful stories of innocent people paying a terrible price, because others have remained silent..." Ellie let her voice trail off ominously, then she gave a bright smile and said in a cheerful voice: "But that shouldn't happen to Sol, should it? After all, he's lucky to have the support of people like his daughter and *you*," she said, subtly stressing the "you." "So I'm sure he'll be fine."

Leaving Ava staring after her, Ellie turned and walked out of the restaurant.

Chapter Twenty-Five

When Ellie finally returned to the villa, she found a note with Aunt Olive's bold scrawl waiting for her on the coffee table.

Have popped over to marina to see Earl. Having dinner with him and might go on a midnight fishing trip afterwards. Don't wait up for me!

Aunt O

XXX

Ellie smiled to herself, wondering if

her aunt was feeling a bit guilty after her various flirtations with other men. As it happened, Ellie was glad to have some time alone that evening. She knew that Aunt Olive would have wanted to pump her for the salacious details of her talk with Blake in the lobby earlier. She still felt raw from their very public "fight" and the last thing she wanted was a post-mortem of the whole sorry affair, no matter how well meaning her aunt might be.

In fact, Ellie had been grateful that the various encounters with Mr. Papadopoulos and then Ava afterwards had distracted her and given her no chance to think about Blake or mull over their argument. She was determined to keep her mind off him now as well. Going to her own room, she had a hot shower, glad to finally have the chance to wash off the sweat and grime from the hot afternoon at the alligator farm. Then, dressed in a comfy old T-shirt and cotton shorts, Ellie flopped onto the couch in the living room and perused the room service menu. She was just trying to decide between the Flame-Grilled Burger with Parmesan Fries and the Florida Crab Cakes with Fresh Lemon and Cilantro Lime Aioli when she heard a scratching noise.

Ellie looked up to see a black whiskered face on the other side of the glass doors leading out onto the private terrace. It was Mojito. The resort cat looked hopefully at Ellie and scratched the glass again. Ellie hesitated, then got up and slid the door open.

"I don't think I'm supposed to be letting you in, you know," she said as the cat strolled into the living room.

"*MIAOW!*" said Mojito with a complacent look as she jumped up on the couch and immediately made herself comfortable on one of the cushions.

Ellie gave a laugh and shook her head.

She had to admire the way cats always had such *chutzpah* and acted like they owned the place. She was about to sit down next to Mojito when she heard the sound of flapping wings behind her.

"Oh no, let me guess," she muttered, turning around. Sure enough, there was an enormous scarlet macaw perched on the lounge chair on the terrace. Hemingway cocked his head and eyed Ellie inquisitively, then he flew down to the ground and walked through the open terrace door.

"OY! YOU PLONKER!" he said as he waddled past Ellie.

"Hemingway!" she gasped. "Why can't you ever repeat nice things?"

"BROCCOLI," said the parrot. "NASTY BROCCOLI."

Ellie sighed, trying not to laugh. "Well, I don't know if that's really saying a 'nice thing' but... I'll take it!"

After the animals turned up, she had

to admit that her mood improved enormously. It was hard to stay glum when faced with Mojito and Hemingway's antics. Somehow, they had a way of making her forget her troubles—if only for a moment—and bringing a smile to her face again. Ellie knew that she probably shouldn't have let the parrot come into the villa, but he looked so cute and comical (especially the way he was waddling across the floor) that she didn't really have the heart to say no.

Besides, as she settled back down on the couch—with Mojito curled up next to her and Hemingway now perched on the couch's arm—she had to admit that there was something really lovely about the animal company. It was companionship without any pressure. They didn't expect her to make conversation; they didn't ask awkward questions about Blake; they just offered easy camaraderie. Mojito purred and kneaded the cushion while Hemingway preened his tail feathers, and Ellie smiled at the thought of a cozy evening ahead with their quiet and soothing presence.

Well, the "quiet" part only lasted about a minute. Then Hemingway seemed to lose interest in his feathers and started looking around for some mischief. He hopped across the back of the couch until he reached the cabinet beside the TV, then hauled himself up using his beak until he was level with the top shelf. There were various books and ornaments on the shelf, including a pair of candleholders carved out of driftwood and a porcelain statue in the shape of a mermaid. Hemingway picked up one of the candleholders in one claw and began nibbling on it. Splinters of wood littered down on the floor beneath the shelf.

"Hey! Don't do that!" Ellie cried, jumping up and snatching it from him.

Hemingway reached for the matching

candleholder and Ellie snatched that out of reach as well. She turned away to put them both on another bookcase across the room. When she turned back, though, she was horrified to see that Hemingway had turned his attention to the porcelain mermaid. He nudged it with his beak, pushing it until it teetered precariously at the edge of the shelf.

"*HEMINGWAY!*" shrieked Ellie. She lunged across the room and caught the mermaid just in time before it tumbled off and smashed on the floor.

"Ooh—you little beast!" she fumed. "If you don't behave yourself, I'm going to kick you back out!"

"KEEP YOUR FEATHERS ON," said the macaw.

Ellie glowered at the parrot. She was just about to answer when someone frantically knocked on the villa door. Surprised, Ellie hurried to open it. She was taken aback to find Jasmine standing on the threshold. After the showdown earlier with Blake, the last person she wanted to deal with was the woman he had been seeing behind her back! She was about to give the girl a curt excuse and shut the door in her face, when she noticed that Jasmine was breathing heavily, as if she had been running, and looked distressed. Before she could ask what the matter was, Jasmine demanded:

"What did you say to Ava?"

"What do you mean?" asked Ellie, surprised.

"She called me and she was, like, totally freaking out! She said you blamed her for getting Dad in trouble. You called her a liar and said she was a coward."

"I never said anything like that!" Ellie protested. "But it sounds to me like Ava has a guilty conscience."

Jasmine started to answer, then

stopped and looked away. Ellie was tempted once again to shut the door in the other girl's face. *After all, this is not my business, not my problem*, she reminded herself. But something about Jasmine's anxiety was beginning to affect her. She felt a stab of guilt as she wondered if she had been too hard on Ava.

"Jasmine... what's really going on?" she asked. "Ava wouldn't be 'freaking out' so badly if she didn't have something to hide. All I did was ask her about the apron that was wrapped around the empty Scorpion Bowl. I said I hope they find the real person who hid it, so that your father doesn't end up being the 'fall guy.' Why should Ava feel so defensive?"

"She's not defensive! She's—" Once again, Jasmine broke off.

Ellie gave her an impatient look. It was so obvious that the other girl knew something. "Look, I know Ava's your best friend, Jasmine, but are you really willing to let your father be convicted for a crime he didn't commit, just to protect her?"

Jasmine remained silent.

"She won't be able to hide forever, you know," said Ellie. "It'll all come out in the end. I'm sure the police will discover the truth eventually. For one thing, I have a duty to tell them my suspicions. I was hoping that Ava would speak up herself, but if she won't, I'm not going to stay silent."

Ellie paused, hoping that the other girl would respond, but Jasmine kept her eyes firmly fixed on the floor. Ellie felt a prickle of irritation and her voice hardened. "I *know* that Ava isn't as innocent as she says. I think *she* was the one who removed the empty Scorpion Bowl, which probably means that she was also the one who poisoned Saunders—"

Jasmine's head jerked up. "*What?* You think Ava murdered that rich guy?"

"Didn't she?" Ellie challenged her.

"*NO!* Jeez, are you crazy? Ava would never murder anyone!"

"Then why is she acting so guilty and scared?" Ellie demanded. She looked the other girl hard in the eyes. "Why is Ava 'freaking out,' as you say, if she's completely innocent?"

"Because she—" Jasmine broke off. Her eyes darted left and right, as if she was thinking rapidly, then she took a deep breath and looked back at Ellie. "OK! Ava *did* take the Scorpion Bowl, all right? She wrapped it up in my Dad's apron and stuffed it into a big plant pot near the building. But that's all she did. She had nothing to do with the murder of the rich dude or poisoning him or whatever. She just took the empty cocktail bowl away after she found his body."

"But why on earth would she do that?" asked Ellie.

"Because she was scared, OK? She thought that if the police found the Scorpion Bowl, they'd suspect her because she served him the cocktail. She thought if she got rid of it, they wouldn't link his death to her."

"But…" Ellie shook her head in bewilderment. "Surely Ava realized they could have linked her in other ways? I mean, whether or not the Scorpion Bowl was found with Saunders's body, the autopsy would have shown that he was poisoned and that the drug was contained in the cocktail that was in his stomach. Then once the police interviewed some witnesses, they would have heard that Ava served him the cocktail—so they would have made the connection anyway!"

"Yeah, well, I guess it was a dumb thing to do," admitted Jasmine. "But you do dumb things, sometimes, when you're scared, right?"

Bloody hell, you can say that again, thought Ellie. Then she said: "Wait—why was Ava in Walter Saunders's suite in the first place?"

"She went to apologize," said Jasmine. "Ava totally lost her sh—I mean, she got really mad 'cos Saunders was such a jerk and his wife was a total witch, but after she cooled off, she got worried that they might, like, complain to the resort management and get her in trouble. See, she's really desperate to get this apprenticeship with the resort and she was scared that she might lose her chance. So she decided to stop by Saunders's room after she finished her shift and, like, apologize... you know, try and patch things up."

Jasmine shook her head. "Talk about bad timing! If Ava had never gone to apologize, she would never have found his body and never gotten involved in the whole mess! She said the door was ajar and when she walked in, she found Saunders on the floor. She went over to check if he was really dead, then she saw the empty Scorpion Bowl on the floor and she panicked. She grabbed it, wrapped it in the apron she was wearing—which happened to be my Dad's, 'cos he lent it to her—and then she got the hell out of there. She was gonna find someplace far away to dump the Scorpion Bowl but then she crashed into you as soon as she came out of the building—"

"And she dropped the bowl," said Elli, thinking that the rest had happened exactly as she'd guessed. "Ava picked it up again when I went into Saunders's suite, but since I was there, she didn't have time to do what she originally planned."

Jasmine nodded. "Yeah, Ava only had, like, a couple of minutes alone when you went ahead, so she had to find some place to hide the bowl fast. That's why she stuffed it into the plant pot. She was gonna go back for it later. But then the police found it—"

"And I identified it as belonging to Sol, which meant that it could be linked back to her," said Ellie, remembering the events of that night. "No wonder Ava looked so scared! I thought she was just traumatized by the experience of finding the body, but no, she was actually terrified of being found out as the person who had removed what was effectively the 'murder weapon'!"

"She's still terrified! She hung up on me in the middle of our call and she wouldn't pick up when I called back. I just went to *Hammerheads* and Ava wasn't there. They said she barely started her shift and then she said she had to go." Jasmine bit her lip. "I'm super worried about her now. You should've heard her on the phone. She was really freaked out and saying all sorts of wild things... I'm scared she'll do something crazy and get hurt!"

Now Jasmine's distress was really becoming infectious. Ellie felt even more guilty as she wondered if her chat with Ava earlier had pushed the girl over the edge.

"Do you know where she might have gone?" she asked.

"No, that's why I'm here!" said Jasmine. "I thought maybe she said something to you?"

Ellie shook her head. "She would hardly talk to me. Is there someone else that she could have gone to? Like her grandmother, maybe?"

"Are you kidding? Ava's grandmother is a strict old bat! She doesn't even approve of Ava wearing dangling earrings! And she'd kill Ava if she ever found out that she'd been, like, rude to a customer or gotten mixed up in a murder."

"Well, what about other friends?"

asked Ellie. "I know you're Ava's best friend, but doesn't she have anyone else she might talk to when she's feeling worried and scared?"

"I guess... maybe her new guy, Sam," said Jasmine with a sour expression. "She's, like, always going on about him... like, how cool and awesome he is. When I was talking to her earlier, she kept saying Sam would know what to do, 'cos he always knows how to sort out trouble at the farm—"

"Wait—did you say Sam works at a farm? What kind of farm?" asked Ellie.

"It's this gator place. It's, like, a few miles from here—"

"Oh my God!" gasped Ellie. "Are you telling me that Ava is dating the manager at Groovy Gator Farm?"

Chapter Twenty-Six

Jasmine looked at Ellie in surprise. "Yeah, that's the dude. Why?"

Ellie thought of the scowling, hard-eyed man she had met. There had been something sinister and menacing about him. Roy Mack might not have had anything to do with Saunders's death, but she wouldn't put it past his farm manager to be involved.

"You've got to get hold of Ava—tell her to stay away from Sam," she said quickly.

"I've told her, like, a hundred times!" said Jasmine in exasperation. "She just won't listen. I've told her that he gives me the creeps and I hate the way he orders her around, but she thinks he's really cool. She says it's awesome how Sam always knows what he wants and isn't afraid to do what it takes to get it."

Like commit murder? wondered Ellie uneasily.

"Do you think Ava could be in danger? From Sam?" asked Jasmine, obviously reading Ellie's expression and jumping to her own conclusions.

"I don't know," said Ellie. "I just... I think he *could* be involved with Saunders's murder but—"

"Omigod! What if Ava starts asking him about it and he's like: she knows too much? Maybe he'll decide he's gotta silence her!" gasped Jasmine. "Omigod, he's gonna kill her!"

"Now, hang on, hang on, don't get carried away—"

"We gotta find her!" cried Jasmine.

"We gotta find Ava and warn her!"

"Well, we don't know if she's in immediate danger," said Ellie, trying to calm the other girl down. "Besides, you said you don't know where she is—"

"She's gone to the gator farm! She kept saying she had to talk to Sam... He lives at the farm, you know. So that must be where she went!"

Jasmine whirled and would have run off if Ellie hadn't reached out and grabbed her arm.

"Wait! Where are you going?" she asked.

Jasmine tried to pull her arm free. "I gotta go to the farm! I gotta go find Ava!"

"What? You can't go to the farm now!"

"Why not?"

"Well, for one thing... it's... it's probably closed," said Ellie inanely.

Jasmine waved a hand. "I know a side

way in. Ava told me about it. It's how she always goes to meet Sam. You don't think she's gonna go through the main gate and pay a ticket to get in every time, do you?"

"OK, but... if you really think that Ava might be in danger, then we should call the police—"

"The cops!" Jasmine's lips curled with scorn. "No way! I'm not gonna call the cops! They're just a bunch of losers. They won't believe us—or they'll make us answer a ton of questions and write statements and stuff. Besides, what are we gonna tell them? How are we gonna explain unless we tell them everything? They don't know about Ava taking the bowl, the resort doesn't know, nobody knows yet. But if we call the cops, we're gonna have to come clean and then Ava will get into a heap of trouble for lying to them. I'm not going to snitch on her—"

"OK, fine! But if you won't involve the police, then at least take someone with you. Maybe your father could—"

"No! Dad's already suffered so much 'cos he was trying to protect Ava. I don't want him to worry even more. Besides, he has to stay at the resort until the cops say he can leave."

"Well, OK, how about..." Ellie swallowed. "How about Blake then? Call him and get him to go with you. At least you'll have a man with you, in case anything happens—"

"Blake's out of town," said Jasmine dismissively. "He was going to Orlando this evening for some medical conference thing. Anyway, he's such a stick-in-the-mud, it would be almost as bad as calling the cops."

Ellie stared at the other girl. It seemed like a strange way to talk about your boyfriend. In fact, Jasmine's entire attitude toward Blake seemed coldly dismissive. *It's none of my business*, she reminded herself, shoving thoughts of

Blake away.

"Well… erm… you can't go to the gator farm alone," said Ellie. She hesitated, then said: "I'll come with you."

"OK. Yeah. Whatever," said Jasmine with a shrug. She tugged her arm out of Ellie's grasp. "Come on! We gotta hurry!"

Ten minutes later, they were in Jasmine's car and turning out of the resort, onto the boulevard which ran past the main entrance. The wide road ran parallel to the beach, past several resorts in a row, as it traversed the length of the barrier island. Several smaller roads branched off from the boulevard, running across the island and leading to bridges which crossed the Intercoastal Waterway back to the main Pinellas County peninsula.

Jasmine drove wildly, with more focus on speed than safety, and Ellie braced herself in her seat while clutching the handle in the door next to her. She was relieved when the alligator farm came into sight. To her surprise, though, Jasmine didn't stop outside the main gate but continued around the corner, taking a smaller road which ran around the property. The road soon merged with a dirt track surrounded by dense vegetation. There were large sections of natural woodland surrounding the farm's perimeter and hardly any other buildings in sight. It was a lot darker too, as there were no street lights here—only the weak headlights of Jasmine's beat-up old Ford wavering on the dirt track in front of them

Finally, they pulled up next to a section of chain-link fence and Jasmine was out of the car almost before the engine stopped. Ellie followed her more slowly, watching as the other girl ran up to the fence and fiddled with something next to the frame. The next moment, a section of the fence swung inwards.

"Come on!" Jasmine beckoned impatiently to Ellie before diving into the undergrowth on the other side of the fence and disappearing from sight.

"Jasmine—wait!" called Ellie, rushing after her.

She ducked through the small opening in the fence and pushed through the shrubs and grasses on the other side, until she stepped out onto a small path. Ellie looked left and right, trying to decide which way to go. On one side, the path headed in the direction of the main gate. On the other, it meandered deeper into the undergrowth. Jasmine was nowhere in sight. Ellie hesitated, then took the direction heading toward the main gate. She walked quickly, hoping to catch up with the other girl soon.

The path led to an open space. It was almost like a farmyard, with a series of low buildings and barns scattered around. The area was poorly lit, with only a few small lights attached to the exterior of the buildings, but luckily there was a full moon that night and it cast a silvery glow across the whole landscape. Ellie paused beside one of the buildings and peered around. The place seemed to be deserted. Had all the farm staff gone home for the day? But no, Jasmine had said that Sam lived on-site, and perhaps other employees did too. Then Ellie remembered the poster of the fundraiser event that Aunt Olive had seen. It was being held in downtown St. Pete. *Was that tomorrow evening or tonight?* She couldn't remember. If it was tonight, perhaps a lot of the farm staff—as well as Roy Mack himself— were at the event.

As Ellie gazed around once more, she realized suddenly that she was in the "backstage" area that Sam had shown her and Mr. Know-It-All during the tour earlier that day. She tried to recall where they had walked in order to orient herself, so she could find the gate that led to the boardwalk. If she could find that, at least she'd be able to follow the outside of the brushwood fence around the perimeter of the lagoon and eventually find her way to the public path, which led to the farm gate.

She saw a section of brushwood fencing up between two buildings ahead of her and started eagerly toward it. But Ellie had barely reached it when she heard voices. Instinctively, she ducked around the corner of a small shed that was next to the fencing. Pressing herself against the side of the structure, she peeked out.

Ellie's heart skipped a beat as she saw Jasmine being marched past by two men. Then her eyes widened in horror. One of them was Sam and he was holding a gun.

Chapter Twenty-Seven

"Take your hands off me!" snapped Jasmine, twisting away as one of the men tried to catch hold of her arm.

"Don't try any funny business," he warned her.

"Oh man... you're like some cheesy movie cliché!" said Jasmine, rolling her eyes. "Where did you learn that line? *Scooby-Doo*? You think that's gonna scare me—"

"Shut up and keep walking," Sam cut in, his voice low but ominous.

Jasmine looked as if she was going to argue, then her eyes flickered to the gun in the farm manager's hand and she thought better of it. Scowling, she turned and continued walking. The men followed close behind.

Ellie felt as if her heart had risen into her throat and was lodged there. She wondered frantically what to do. Should she confront them? Her first instinct was to rush out and help Jasmine, but she restrained herself. After all, she was unarmed and hardly a match for two grown men—and she wasn't going to do the girl any good if she got caught as well. But if she did nothing, she'd be abandoning Jasmine to her captors, and who knew what they might do to her?

Ellie shifted her weight from foot to foot as she agonized over what to do. She could leave and go for help... but if she did that, she wouldn't know where they were taking Jasmine. What if she came back with the police and the girl was nowhere to be seen? Sam and the other man could deny that they knew anything and it would be their word against hers.

What do I do? What do I do? she wondered frantically. Then she mentally smacked her head. *Duh! Why didn't I think of it before? I can use my phone to call for help!* She dug in her shorts pocket but before she could pull her cellphone out, she heard the group approaching. She shoved her phone back into her pocket and retreated farther around the side of the shed as they came closer. She backed up until she felt something hard and bristly press against her back. Glancing around, Ellie realized that she had backed up against the brushwood fencing. She gulped. If the men came around the side of the shed, she would have nowhere else to retreat to.

Ellie looked around in a panic. She was hemmed in on either side by buildings, and behind her was the brushwood fencing. The only place of refuge was a gnarled tree beside her. It had spreading branches covered by a dense canopy, stretching over both sides of the fence. Ellie looked at the thick trunk doubtfully. She had climbed trees a lot as a little girl—it was her favorite thing to do when her mother used to take her to Hyde Park back in London—but she hadn't attempted any arboreal acrobatics for years. She had no idea if she could still do it.

Still, the sound of approaching footsteps decided it for her. Ellie hesitated for a split second, then lunged at the lowest branch. She grabbed it and hauled herself up. For a moment, she hung in midair, grappling with the branch, the knobby wood digging into her stomach and her legs flailing below. Then she managed to twist her body, hook one leg over the branch, and pull her weight up. Panting with effort, she raised herself to sit astride the branch.

And not a moment too soon. Sam and

the other man came around the side of the shed, with Jasmine between them. Ellie yanked her legs up quickly, so that they wouldn't dangle below the canopy and be seen. She shrank back, wondering if she was hidden enough. If the men looked up into the tree, would they see her? Feeling too exposed, Ellie shuffled backward and crawled across onto another branch, which stretched over the other side of the fence. Carefully, she made her way out along the second branch, until she was well over the other side of the brushwood fencing. She felt safer now, since she was no longer above the men's heads.

She peered through the leaves. The men had stopped beside the shed and seemed to be discussing something. Their voices were too low for Ellie to hear properly. Jasmine stood next to them with her arms folded across her chest and a scowl across her face. Ellie was puzzled. The other girl looked oddly calm for someone who had been captured and was being held hostage. In fact, she looked more like a bored teenager annoyed with a parent for picking her up late! And when the men finally stopped talking and started escorting her again, she shook their hands off and stalked ahead of them with her nose in the air.

The trio disappeared around the corner of another building and Ellie heard the men's voices fading into the distance. They seemed to be going in the direction of the main gate. As soon as they were out of sight, she sagged in relief. Then she remembered the call she was going to make. Quickly, Ellie pulled her cellphone out of her pocket and scrabbled for the dial pad with clumsy fingers, trying to press: 9...9...9...

Then she stopped herself. *Nooo! 999 is the emergency number for the U.K.! What's the number to call for emergencies in America? What? What?* Her mind went blank. *Was it 911? That's what's in all the Hollywood movies... isn't it?*

She groped for the dial screen again, but her hands fumbled over the phone's slick surface and it slipped from her fingers, falling to the ground below.

"Oh bugger!" muttered Ellie, leaning over to peer down.

She could see the phone lying on the ground right beneath the branch, its smooth screen gleaming as it reflected the light from the moon. Then she noticed an echoing shimmer of reflected light nearby and realized that it came from a large pool of water. Ellie sat up and took a good look around for the first time. She realized that she was looking down into the enclosure which contained the main alligator lagoon. She had completely forgotten that it was on the other side of the brushwood fencing. The spreading branches of the tree had stretched over both sides of the fence and the branch she was sitting on was arched over the enclosure.

The water from the lagoon lapped close to where her phone had dropped onto the bank. The area was surrounded by overgrown plants and large boulders, but no alligators, as far as Ellie could see. She took a deep breath and leaned down, stretching her arm as far out as she could to try and reach her phone. But it was no good. No matter how hard she strained, her fingertips always fell short by a few inches.

Ellie sighed and sat up again. What should she do? She needed her phone to call for help, otherwise she would have to leave the farm, and that would mean leaving Jasmine. She was already worried about where the men were taking the other girl. She had hoped to follow them and keep Jasmine in sight. This fiasco with her phone was already delaying her.

She looked back at the ground. It wasn't that far below her—in fact, the branch drooped even lower at its far end. If she crawled out to the end of the branch, she could easily jump off, run across to her phone, pick it up, then run back to the branch and climb up again. The whole thing wouldn't take more than a few minutes.

But it *would* mean jumping down into an enclosure filled with alligators. Ellie swallowed. Did she dare risk it?

She looked carefully around again. The area below her seemed to be clear. Then she had a bright idea: she reached out and broke off several short twigs from the branch she was sitting on. Taking careful aim, she threw each of these at different shapes on the bank below her. Nothing moved. *OK, surely if any of those were alligators, they would have reacted?* she told herself.

Feeling reassured, Ellie began crawling out to the end of the branch. Her weight bent it even more so that by the time she reached the end, it had drooped almost to the ground. She took a deep breath, glanced around once more, then dropped off the branch onto the bank beneath.

It was softer than she had expected, and the sandy texture shifted beneath her feet. Ellie bit off a cry of surprise and flung out her arms to steady herself. She regained her balance and looked quickly around, her heart pounding.

But all was quiet around her. Nothing rustled, nothing moved, nothing slithered across the sand. Ellie relaxed slightly. *It'll be fine*, she told herself. *Alligators probably sleep at night anyway.* She just had to run across, grab her phone, then come back here and haul herself back onto the branch.

Moving as silently as she could, Ellie ran across the sandy bank to where her phone was lying. She was just bending to scoop it up when she heard a sound behind her and froze.

A low, menacing hiss.

It was coming from behind her. Ellie whirled around and saw something dark emerge from the ripples at the edge of the lagoon. Water streamed off the long, scaley snout and armored body. The moonlight glinted in the cold yellow eyes.

Ellie forgot to breathe as she stood and stared at the enormous alligator rising out of the water.

Chapter Twenty-Eight

The alligator paused at the edge of the lagoon and opened its jaws slightly, revealing rows of yellowed teeth.

Oh my God, oh my God, oh my God, thought Ellie. She had been so fixated on the shore that she had completely forgotten about the water. How could she have been so stupid? Hadn't she listened to the tour guide earlier that afternoon at all? Alligators were ambush predators. They lay in wait in the water, keeping perfectly still, with only their eyes protruding above the surface. And when the unsuspecting prey came along…

Ellie looked desperately around and saw with horror that the alligator was between her and "her" tree branch. In order to run back and climb up to safety, she would have to run straight past the alligator's open jaws.

Uh-uh… no way, she thought. But that meant that her escape route was cut off. The tree branch had been her means of climbing back out of the enclosure. How was she going to get out now?

Come on, think! Think! she told herself frantically. It was hard to focus, though, when a huge reptile was smiling at you with all of its eighty teeth.

The gator took a few more steps, hauling itself out of the water, its belly making a rasping sound as it slid along the sand. It turned its head slowly, as if scenting the air, and looked myopically at her.

Ellie swallowed and shifted her weight

onto the balls of her feet, poised to jump. Even as she had the thought, the alligator moved. It lunged forward with another hiss. Ellie yelped and sprang back, nearly losing her balance. The gator's jaws snapped around something in the sand, where she had been standing a moment ago. There was a metallic crunching sound.

"No!" Ellie gasped. "That's my phone!"

The alligator looked slightly confused. It mouthed the phone, moving the device between its teeth, then slowly opened and shut its jaws, as if chewing a very large wad of sticky bubble gum. Ellie winced as she heard more crunching.

"Nooo…" she groaned. "How am I going to call for help now?"

"*How can I help you? I'm listening,*" said the alligator.

"Huh?" Ellie stared at the reptile.

It looked back at her, grinning

stupidly. Then it tipped its head back and made a gulping motion. Faint electronic beeps came from its mouth. Ellie saw the muscles of its throat move up and down.

"Great, now you've swallowed it," she muttered.

"*You can swallow anything if it's seasoned with enough praise,*" said the gator.

"Whaaat?"

"*The polite way to ask someone to repeat themselves is: Pardon me?*"

"Oh my God, this isn't happening to me," Ellie moaned, passing a hand over her face.

"*It is debatable whether your awareness of an event is proof of its existence. However, Descartes's dictum: Cogito, ergo sum—I think, therefore I am—suggests that in order to be doubted, an event must exist in the first place.*"

"This is insane," muttered Ellie. "I can't believe I'm stuck in a lagoon, having a conversation with an alligator about the meaning of existence." She shook her head. "And now I'm talking to myself. I must sound like a complete loony... oh wait, what do they call it in America? A total wacko!"

"Sure, I can call you a taco. There are six restaurants serving tacos in the local area. Which would you like me to call?"

Ellie was beginning to feel a hysterical urge to laugh. Then the alligator moved and she was suddenly brought back to reality with a thump. If she didn't get out of there, she would soon be joining her phone in the gator's belly. The gator moved slowly toward her, its claws digging into the sand. Ellie backed away, conscious that the brushwood fencing was only a few yards behind her. Once she was up against it, there would be nowhere else to go. The fencing was tall, with no gaps and no easy grips for climbing, and it was too solid to break easily. There were no other tree branches that stretched low over the shore, which she could use to climb out of the enclosure.

Then her eyes lit on a wooden structure a short distance away. Of course! The boardwalk! If she could climb up onto that, she'd be safely out of reach and she'd be able to walk across the lagoon and back onto the public path which led to the entrance.

It would mean having to cross a short stretch of shore, though. Ellie eyed the distance in front of her doubtfully. It looked like it was strewn with rocks and boulders, old logs and swamp plants. But it was hard to make out shapes clearly, even in the bright moonlight. There were too many shadows and gray forms, and she couldn't be a hundred percent certain if those shapes were logs and boulders or large reptiles.

But I can't just stand here either,

waiting to be eaten! thought Ellie, glancing back at the alligator. It had stopped moving toward her, and was making electronic hiccupping noises. Maybe it was getting iPhone indigestion. Or maybe it was just gathering itself and getting ready to lunge again. *Well, I'm not hanging around to find out!*

"See you later, alligator," she muttered.

Then she turned and sprinted for the boardwalk. She raced past rocks and logs, kicking up sand and rustling through tall grasses. She heard hisses and growls coming from the lagoon, and the sound of ominous splashing, as her sudden movements disturbed the main group of alligators in the water. More of them would be coming soon to check out the disturbance. If she didn't manage to climb up onto the boardwalk, she was going to be in big trouble.

Ellie arrived at the base of one of the supporting poles and threw herself at it.

She had often read the phrase "fear gives you wings"—well, she didn't know about wings, but it certainly gave you superhuman strength! She found herself shimmying up the pole like a monkey and, in a minute, she could reach the wooden railing with her fingers. Gasping and panting, she hauled herself up and over, tumbling over the railing and collapsing in a heap on the boardwalk.

She lay for a moment, trying to catch her breath and still the crazy thumping of her heart. Her legs felt like jelly and she was shaking with relief. Finally, she rolled over and used the railing to pull herself to her feet. She leaned against the side of the boardwalk and looked back down at the enclosure below. There were several half-submerged shapes gliding through the water toward the shore. In the distance, the first alligator was still staring stupidly at the spot where she had been. Faintly, she could hear an electronic voice saying:

"...originated in American teenage slang, is a catchphrase used on parting. The expected response is: in a while, crocodile!"

Ellie was suddenly hit by a fit of the giggles and, once she started laughing, she couldn't stop. All the pent-up panic and hysteria turned into helpless laughter and she leaned against the railing, gasping for breath as she tried to control herself.

Then she felt a hand on her shoulder.

Ellie choked and whirled around, fear clamping around her throat again. A man was standing on the boardwalk behind her. She had been laughing so hard that she hadn't heard him walking up. The light from the moon fell on his features and Ellie suddenly recognized his face. It was Roy Mack, the alligator farm owner. He was looking at her with concern, his brow furrowed in puzzlement.

"Ma'am... are you OK? What are you doing here?" he asked.

"I..." Ellie was lost for words. What should she say?

Recognition flickered in Mack's face. "Hey, you're that lady who was here earlier this afternoon with that other man. Sam gave you guys a private tour, right?" He frowned. "The farm is closed to visitors now. Did you somehow get locked in?"

"No, I..." Again, Ellie broke off, unsure what to do. Should she tell him? Could she trust him?

She thought back to the conversation she had overheard earlier and her impression that Roy Mack was not a suspect after all. He could be a big help in finding his farm manager and rescuing Jasmine, if she could get him on her side.

Impulsively, Ellie grabbed his arm and said, "I need your help! Your farm manager Sam—I think he's involved in the murder of your business partner. He's... erm... kidnapped a friend of mine. I need you to help me save her!"

"*What?*" Roy Mack stared at her as if she'd gone mad.

"I know it sounds crazy but I'm not making it up," Ellie insisted. "Sam had a gun and he was taking my friend away. I'm worried about what he might do to her. We've got to find them quickly!"

"Why do you think he would harm your friend?"

"Because he wants to silence her! He's worried that she might know too much and he doesn't want his part in Saunders's murder to come out—"

Roy Mack laughed. "I think your imagination is running away with you, ma'am."

"No, you have to listen to me, please! He—"

"I came through the main gate myself a short while ago and I saw Sam personally escorting a young black woman off the premises. Was that your friend?"

"Yes, that's Jasmine..." Ellie faltered, bewildered. "You saw Sam let her go? Are you sure?"

"Sure, I'm sure. Sam wasn't hurting her in any way. He just wanted to make sure that she wasn't roaming around the farm by herself. We keep dangerous animals here, you know, and we can't allow members of the public to have free access, in case they enter enclosures and injure themselves or the reptiles."

"Oh." Ellie felt like the wind had been taken out of her sails. *Could she have been wrong about everything?*

"Say, why did you think Sam could be involved in Walt's murder? Did your friend tell you that?" asked Mack.

Ellie shook her head urgently. "No,

she was just worried about *her* friend Ava, who is dating Sam. She came here looking for Ava. Jasmine doesn't like Sam very much—she thinks he's a creep—but I think he's more than that. I think he's a murderer! I think he took some diazepam from your supply here at the farm and used it to spike Saunders's cocktail."

"Why the hell would he want to do that?"

"I don't know... maybe... maybe Sam felt threatened by your business partner. Saunders was going to come and inspect the farm, wasn't he? I... erm... I overheard the two of you talking on the day you came to see him at the resort," said Ellie, giving Roy Mack an embarrassed look. "I was sitting at the table next to you, on the other side of the big potted palm—"

"You were spying on us?"

"Oh no, not on purpose! I just

happened to be sitting there already when you arrived and I overheard your meeting. I know Saunders wasn't happy about something to do with the farm accounts and he was threatening to come and do a personal audit."

"You heard a lot for someone who wasn't eavesdropping on purpose."

Ellie flushed. "It was an accident."

"Just like it was an accident that you were spying on me and Sam earlier today?"

"I wasn't! Honestly, I was just curious about what was on the other side of the brushwood fencing and it so happened that you and Sam walked past and you were talking…" Ellie trailed off, then she took a deep breath and said, "Anyway, I'm really sorry to have caused all this bother. It looks like maybe I was wrong about Sam after all. I must have… erm… misunderstood things. If you'll just show me to the front entrance, I'll get off the property and leave you in peace."

Mack smiled at her. "I'm afraid I can't do that."

Ellie felt a chill. "Why not?"

"Well, you see, unlike your friend, you *do* know too much."

Ellie licked dry lips. "Wh...what d'you mean? I thought you said that I'd jumped to the wrong conclusions—"

Mack's smile widened. "Well, sorta. You were right that Walt was poisoned by the diazepam which we use here for the gators... you were just wrong about the guy who did it." He leaned toward her. "*I* was the one who spiked the Scorpion Bowl. *I* murdered Walter Saunders."

Chapter Twenty-Nine

Ellie stared at the man in front of her. She felt as if she should have known all along, and yet it was as if her mind was rejecting the fact. *No, no, it can't be Roy Mack...*

"But... but you can't have," she said weakly. "I saw you put that dried scorpion in Saunders's drink, but that was all. There was nothing else in your hand. I was watching you the whole time!"

Roy Mack laughed and raised his right hand with a flourish. "That's what the audiences always say. Believe me, as someone who's done a lot of shows in his time, I can tell you that people are *never* watching you the whole time. Especially," he raised his left hand as well, "when it's your *other* hand that's doing the important stuff. Yeah, that's right—the hand that nobody is watching. I'll bet you were keeping your eyes on the hand holding the dried scorpion the whole time, weren't you? Sure you were! Who wouldn't be? It's the kinda thing that's guaranteed to attract attention: seeing some guy add a creepy bug to someone else's cocktail." He chuckled. "I was counting on that. I knew that if anyone was watching, they'd focus on that part and not notice what my other hand was doing as I leaned over."

Mack gave her a smug smile. "It's the basic principle of sleight-of-hand: misdirection. I learned it all back when I was practicing for magic shows, see? It's all about keeping up the patter, keeping your audience entertained and engaged, hiding the smaller movements with the larger movements... in this case, keeping everyone's attention on my right hand while I use my other hand to pull off the trick."

Ellie's mind whirled. She suddenly remembered the other half of the conversation she'd had with Earl during that fishing trip. After they'd discussed the myths surrounding alligators, he'd told her a bit about Roy Mack's background: "*...he used to be on the circuit in downtown St. Pete—had a regular show doing a mix of stand-up comedy, magic tricks, daredevil stunts, you name it... He left it all behind when he went into the gator farming business...*"

Except that Roy Mack hadn't left it all behind, thought Ellie. He had used his old magician's skills to pull off a daring murder, right under the noses of all the other guests at the resort! *And right under my nose too,* she thought, annoyed with herself.

As if reading her mind, Mack chuckled again and added, "Never would've thought my magician's training would come in handy to protect my business interests one day."

"That's why you killed him? Because Saunders was threatening your business interests?"

"Hell yeah!" said Mack. "That schmuck was gonna destroy everything! He was supposed to be a 'silent partner,' right? He was supposed to give me the money to start up and let me get on with it—not come snooping around, asking awkward questions. Those morons at the FWC have no clue. I wasn't gonna let Walt ruin everything!"

"The FWC?" Ellie said. The only time she'd heard that acronym mentioned recently was when Earl had discussed licenses to harvest alligator eggs from the wild. "Do you mean the Florida Fish and Wildlife Conservation Commission?"

"Yeah, those jerks wouldn't give me a permit. They want me to pay a packet to collect eggs from private land—we're talking like fifty bucks per egg, you know—*and* pay a fee to Uncle Sam for every egg I find. No way!" said Mack angrily. "Meanwhile, the established farms who have the permits get their eggs for cheap from state land. You call that fair?" He shook his head firmly. "Nuh-ah. I don't call that fair. I call that a rip-off! So I decided to just do some harvesting on the sly. Turns out there are professionals out there who do egg poaching as a day job!" He laughed. "And it didn't take a lot of asking around to hook up with them."

"But I don't understand what any of this has to do with Walter Saunders," said Ellie. "Why did you have to kill him?"

"Because if he started kicking up a stink about the numbers not adding up, that might have alerted the FWC. They've already been getting twitchy in recent years about egg poaching and they've been on the lookout for farms reporting hatch rates much higher than 80%. The last thing I need is a bunch of agents coming around and asking me questions. I've got a pretty slick operation now and some good buyers up in Louisiana. Gator eggs can be worth twenty bucks or more each. That's a cool thousand for a nest of fifty eggs," said Mack proudly, sounding like he'd laid the eggs himself. "This past harvest, I had one buyer come down and write me a check for ten grand!"

While the farm owner had been talking, Ellie had been trying to quietly edge away. She hoped that Mack would be so engrossed in his bragging, he wouldn't notice until she was too far away for him to reach out and grab her. Then she could take off and run across the boardwalk to the other side of the lagoon. But even as she shifted her weight, preparing to run, she saw him narrow his eyes suddenly.

"Hey—don't try any funny business," he said, reaching toward his belt.

A minute later, Ellie found herself staring into the muzzle of a revolver.

"Yeah, Sam isn't the only one who has a gun," said Mack, smiling as he saw the expression on her face. "And I won't hesitate to use it. Now, come on— enough talk. Let's get going."

He reached out and grabbed her, hauling her close to him and forcing her to start walking with him along the boardwalk.

"Where... where are we going?" asked Ellie breathlessly.

"Oh, I know a nice little piece of land... very remote... where gators like to make their nests... and where a body won't be found for many weeks," said Mack with a smile.

Ellie felt sick. She wanted to fight, to resist, but somehow her mind felt numb as she stumbled along the boardwalk. All she could think of was how alone she was: her aunt was out with Earl on a boat in the Gulf of Mexico somewhere, Blake was in another city, Sol was under a form of "house arrest" at the resort, and his daughter Jasmine... even if it was true that Sam had let Jasmine go, what would the girl do? Would she worry about Ellie? Or would she just assume that Ellie would look after herself and go off to search for her friend Ava instead?

A wave of despair swamped Ellie. No one was going to come and rescue her. She was on her own. And her only hope now was to get away from Roy Mack. But how? Even if she managed to break free and run, he had a gun. They were on a narrow boardwalk and, unless she wanted to jump back into the lagoon below, she could only run down the boardwalk away from him.

He will just shoot me in the back, thought Ellie miserably. *This is even worse than facing that alligator just now—*

Wait. The thought of facing alligators made something else flicker in her memory. *What did Earl say you should do if you were grabbed by an alligator?* Ellie tried desperately to remember. *Smack it on the snout? Stick your finger in its eyes?*

Well, Roy Mack didn't have a snout, but he did have eyes...

Before she had time to consider whether it was the wisest thing to do, Ellie whirled toward the man next to her. She took Mack by surprise. Her dejected, stumbling walk must have convinced him that she was weak and terrified, and his grip on her had loosened. Now he reeled back with a yell of surprise as she turned and jabbed her thumb into one of his eye sockets.

"AAAGGHHH!"

Mack stumbled back, raising a hand to shield his face. Ellie yanked herself free and took off. She heard him cursing furiously behind her and she felt a flash of fear as she remembered that Mack still had the gun. *They said you shouldn't run in a zigzag when running from a gator—but was it the same when running from a human shooter?* she wondered wildly.

Gunshots sounded in the air.

Ellie made a split-second decision and began zigzagging from side to side as she ran.

Something struck the wooden railing next to her as she raced past, narrowly missing her. Something else whistled past her head.

Ellie kept running, twisting and changing direction constantly, until she reached the end of the boardwalk. She flung herself off the wooden walkway and careened down the path which led toward the main entrance of the farm.

She nearly cried with relief when the path widened into a large courtyard and she saw the buildings holding the farm shop and the café on one side. Beside them were the enormous double gates of the front entrance. But as she rushed up to the big iron structure and flung herself against the metal bars, a new wave of despair swept over her.

The gate was locked!

Ellie shook it as hard as she could. The metal scraped and rattled, but it remained firmly bolted shut, with a padlocked chain reinforcing the bolts. She tried shouting but she knew that the gator farm was situated on the outskirts of town. There were no shopping malls or busy streets nearby. Would anyone hear her cries for help? She tried nevertheless, all the time conscious that her voice was also telling Mack exactly where she was. The farm owner would be approaching, gun in hand... and somewhere else in the farm, his manager Sam would probably be coming too, attracted by the sound of the gunshots and the commotion from her yells. Ellie sagged against the bars, feeling completely defeated.

She saw a figure appear on the public path. Her heart sank. It was Roy Mack. He was running toward her, brandishing the gun. She cringed back against the gate, feeling like a trapped animal.

Mack rushed up, panting, his face hard and his eyes cold.

He raised the gun. Ellie gasped and shrank back even more.

Then Mack cursed and flung his other arm over his face as he was suddenly blinded by headlights. A car roared up to the other side of the gate, its lights pointing in through the bars. Ellie heard car doors opening and the sound of footsteps running. She turned, blinking, and tried to see, but it was hard to make out anything in the blinding light. She heard a man's voice yell:

"LOWER YOUR WEAPON!"

And then she heard a female voice she recognized. The next minute, she felt hands reach through the bars and clasp her own.

"Ellie! It's OK!" cried Jasmine. "I've brought the police—you're safe!"

Chapter Thirty

"Great gibbons, I can't believe that the whole thing was just about 'poached eggs'!" said Aunt Olive, laughing heartily.

It was "Happy Hour" the next evening and they were sitting side by side in a cabana on the beach, watching the sun go down. The sky in front of them was streaked in a spectacular pattern of vivid pinks and fiery oranges, and the waters of the Gulf rippled with deep purple shadows beneath. Sitting there, with the balmy sea breeze on her face, and the lazy call of the seagulls filling the air, it was hard for Ellie to believe that only the night before, she had been facing a situation of life and death.

Now she threw her aunt a wry look and said, "You know what was the weirdest moment? When I was standing there having a conversation with that bloody alligator! I mean, I felt like I had stepped into an alternate universe!"

"Ah... it seems that your gator friend has become quite the celebrity," said Aunt Olive with a grin.

"What do you mean?"

Aunt Olive reached for her phone and tapped a few times on the screen, then turned it around to show Ellie a video clip recently posted on social media. A female news anchor sat behind a desk:

"...arrests made last night at the Groovy Gator Farm, with the owner and farm manager in custody. However, the reptiles are still being cared for by the remaining staff and the farm has been inundated with visitors today, all eager to see the 'talking gator.' Reports from the keepers this morning claim that one of the gators has spontaneously begun to speak. The ten-foot male responds to questions and will predict the weather, tell you who won last year's Superbowl, and even discuss the meaning of life. Tickets to the farm are selling out fast and families are doing anything to take their kids to see this animal phenomenon."

Ellie shook her head in disbelief as she watched the video showing a crowd of people pushing and shoving against the farm's gates, yelling and waving their phone cameras, trying to see into the park.

"Well, they'd better sell a lot of tickets before the battery runs out on my phone," she said with a dry laugh. "It's unbelievable... Honestly, the whole thing is a total farce!"

"As long as the farce puts Roy Mack

away for a very long time," said Aunt Olive.

"Oh, I think they've got more than enough to nail him. Even if Mack doesn't get convicted for murder in the end, they've still got him for racketeering—and that means a thirty-year prison sentence," said Ellie with satisfaction. "That's the kind of charge usually brought against mobsters and drug cartels, you know! It might sound funny to you, but 'poached eggs' is serious business in Florida. Roy Mack is essentially considered to be part of an 'organized criminal conspiracy.'"

Aunt Olive shook her head. "When you think of organized crime, you think of drugs, counterfeit goods, human trafficking... the last thing you think of is alligator eggs!"

"They fetch good money though," said Ellie. "Detective Carson was telling me last night that there's a black market for gator eggs, especially from buyers in

Louisiana. The whole alligator farm industry is much bigger there, you know—like something over thirty-five million dollars a year! And they just can't get enough eggs, so they'll pay really good money to restock their farms, which they can get more easily from Florida, since there are loads more wild alligators here. But, of course, taking eggs from the wild without a permit is a felony here."

"Hmm, fascinating... I'm beginning to think these points would all make great plot elements for a book. I must do more research into this," mused Aunt Olive. She lifted the cocktail glass by her side and took a sip of her Mai Tai, then threw Ellie a mischievous look. "How about another trip to an alligator farm?"

"No, thank you!" said Ellie with a shudder. "Right now, I feel like I never want to see another alligator ever again! Honestly, Aunt Olive, I think I lost five years off my life when I was running across that lagoon enclosure and trying to climb up onto the boardwalk before the alligators got me."

Aunt Olive chuckled. "Well, you *did* say you wanted more adventure and excitement in your life."

"Oh no, no more adventure and excitement for me," Ellie declared. She leaned back in her lounge chair and yawned tiredly. "You know, I was at the county sheriff's station, answering questions practically all night. I didn't get back to the resort until nearly four in the morning! At the rate I'm going, I'm going to need another vacation to recover from *this* vacation!" Then she frowned and sat up again. "There's one thing that's still puzzling me though."

"What's that, poppet?

"Tonya said that she left Saunders's suite while Rob was still with his uncle, which means that Rob was the last person to see the murdered man alive.

But when I spoke to Rob, he was adamant that *he* left the suite before she did! So according to him, *Tonya* was the last person to see Walter Saunders alive."

"Does it matter? Neither of them are guilty of the murder—" Aunt Olive started to say.

"Yes, I know, but it's still bothering me because it just doesn't make sense! I mean, Rob really did seem to be sincere when he was telling me that he heard Tonya speaking on the phone. I don't think he was lying to me or making something up just to frame her. But then... does that mean that Tonya was lying? Why would she have lied about that? Given that she wasn't involved in Saunders's murder, why would she pretend that she left earlier than she did?"

Aunt Olive had been looking thoughtfully across the beach at the other resort cabanas arranged around them. Now she turned back to Ellie and said with a covert smile: "What exactly did Rob say when he told you that he heard Tonya?"

Ellie furrowed her brow. "He said he heard her talking on her phone, out on the balcony, just as he was leaving. She was talking to a girlfriend, asking what they were doing."

"Did he see her? Or did he only hear her?" asked Aunt Olive.

"I think he only heard her. The balcony wraps around the entire suite, so I suppose Tonya must have been standing farther around the side of the balcony, out of sight of the living room windows."

"Ahhh... well, I have an idea," said Aunt Olive.

She nodded at something a few feet away from them. Ellie turned to follow her aunt's gaze and saw Hemingway the scarlet macaw perched atop the canopy of one of the other cabanas. He was making a racket as usual, bobbing up and down and spreading his wings wide every so often as he hooted and whistled. As Ellie watched, the parrot cocked his head to one side and began mimicking the popular iPhone ringtone: "*Toodoo-da-doo-da-doo-doooo…*"

He sounded so realistic that several people in nearby cabanas began scrabbling around, looking for their phones. The parrot screeched with laughter as a few people actually picked up their devices and said: "Hello? Hello?"

"HELLO? HIYA. WHATCHA DOIN'?" croaked the macaw, copying them.

Ellie shook her head in admiration. "I have to say, he really is an amazing mimic! That ringtone sounded so realistic, and he even copies all the different guests' voices and accents perfectly!"

"Yes, and that's the answer to your

mystery," said Aunt Olive. "I'll bet that it wasn't Tonya that Rob heard out on the balcony—it was Hemingway! Rob said he heard Tonya 'answer a call'—isn't that right? Well, that would fit. He could have heard Hemingway singing the ringtone and then saying 'Hello?' or even 'Whatcha doin'?' in Tonya's voice, which would have sounded like she was chatting to a friend. Since Rob couldn't see, he just assumed that it was her. Meanwhile, she *had* actually left the suite already, but Rob was so engrossed with his uncle, he never noticed. So they were both telling the truth—or at least, what they both thought was the truth."

"Oh my God, I think you're right!" said Ellie in elation. "I've just remembered that on the night of the murder, I was walking on the beach past the Ocean View Wing. I saw Hemingway perched on one of the balconies: he was making ringtone noises and talking to himself... so he could have been there earlier that evening, doing the exact same thing, when Rob was leaving the suite."

"Well, there you have it," said Aunt Olive. "If Hemingway was in the habit of perching on the balconies, he would likely have overheard Tonya talking on her phone before—either through the open windows or maybe when she really went out on the balcony. It would have taken very little for him to start copying her."

Ellie shook her head with affectionate exasperation. "Hemingway always seems to—"

She broke off as she suddenly noticed a couple coming down the path from the main resort complex and crossing the beach toward them. She recognized the tall African-American man and the pretty girl by his side. It was Sol, with Jasmine in tow.

Chapter Thirty-One

"Sol! How nice to see you!" Ellie cried, springing up.

"Ah, have the police released you? About time," said Aunt Olive tartly. "I would have thought that you should have been cleared this morning, Sol."

"Yup, I'm a free man," Sol said, grinning. "They did let me go earlier today but I've been down at the station, answering questions and updating my statement."

"Updating your statement?"

Sol slanted a look at his daughter. "Jasmine here wanted me to set a few things straight with the police."

Ellie wondered what he meant but he didn't elaborate and she didn't feel that it was polite to ask. Her aunt, however, had no such qualms.

"Whatever do you mean, Sol? Do tell!" she said.

"Aunt Olive!" Ellie gave her aunt a reproachful look. "Maybe it's private."

"Oh, fiddle-faddle. If Sol hadn't wanted to be asked about it, then he shouldn't have mentioned it—isn't that right, Sol?" Aunt Olive beamed at him and patted the space next to her on her lounge chair. "Come and sit by me and tell me *every*thing!"

Sol chuckled and Ellie felt her heart warm to hear the familiar rich laugh. He moved to take the seat next to her aunt and, as they started to talk, Ellie felt a gentle tug on her arm and turned to find Jasmine looking earnestly at her.

"Hey... I wanted to say thank you for

helping my Dad."

"Oh, no, if anyone should be thanking anyone, it's me who should be thanking you," Ellie said quickly. "If you hadn't brought the police last night, I would have been a 'goner,' as they say."

Jasmine giggled. "Yeah, I've always wanted to turn up some place and yell: 'Police! Drop your weapon!'—like they do in the movies." She pouted. "Detective Carson wouldn't let me do it last night. It would have been so awesome!"

"By the way, what happened after we split up at the farm? Did Sam catch you? I saw you with him and another man, and I thought they were going to do something terrible to you."

"Nah, Sam just marched me out the gate and told me to get lost. I ran into him when I was searching for Ava. He told me that he and Ava had actually broken up last night. I was like: 'No way!

Ava would have told me!' But he said it was true and he hadn't seen her since last weekend. I still didn't believe him so I started kicking up a stink and shouting Ava's name and stuff. I figured, if he was keeping her there, like, tied up or something, then she'd hear me and know that I was searching for her. But he got really pissed and he took out a gun and started waving it around, like, trying to scare me." Jasmine rolled her eyes. "He said I was trespassing and if I didn't leave, he was gonna deal with me and I was like, yeah, whatever…" She gave a contemptuous wave of her hand. "In the end, I was like: 'Fine, I'm leaving,' and Sam said he would walk me to the gate 'cos he didn't trust me."

"So he just let you go? Just like that?" Ellie shook her head. "I can't believe it. There I was, imagining all sorts of awful things happening to you, and he was just escorting you out of the farm!"

"Yeah, well, I still didn't trust him. As

soon as I got out, I called the cops. I mean, I didn't really want to 'cos, like I told you, they're just a major pain in the neck, but I was kinda worried about you and I didn't know who else to call. Of course, they didn't believe me at first. They thought I was, like, pranking them or something! But then I made them put that detective on. You know, that Carson dude. I managed to convince him to come to the farm."

"Thank God you did," said Ellie fervently. "And what about Ava? Was she OK?"

"Yeah, she didn't go to the farm last night, actually. Sam was telling the truth about that. Ava went back to her Nan's place." Jasmine paused, then added in a more serious tone: "Ava's decided to come clean and tell the police everything. Even if it costs her the apprenticeship here at the resort."

"I don't think it will come to that," said Ellie with a smile. "I have a feeling that

Mr. Papadopoulos will be very understanding."

"You think so?" Jasmine brightened. Then she looked at Ellie curiously. "So… what are you planning to do now?"

"Sleep for three days," said Ellie with a laugh. "I don't know. Just take things easy, I suppose. Laze by the pool, search for seashells on the beach, drink cocktails… Do the things that I came to Florida for!"

Jasmine grinned at Ellie, then said, "You know, you're kinda cool. My Dad says you're staying at the resort until the new year. You wanna hang out sometime? I could show you around the Tampa Bay area."

"Oh… erm…" Ellie was taken aback. She didn't want to admit it, but she had come to like Jasmine. The girl might have been impulsive and immature, but she was also spirited, loyal, and had inherited her father's warm charisma. In any other situation, Ellie would have been glad to make a new friend. But what about Blake? She just couldn't get over seeing Jasmine as "the other woman" and she certainly didn't want to have to spend any time with them together!

"Erm… well, that's really sweet of you." Ellie licked her lips. "But I'm sure you're busy with your own stuff and you wouldn't want to be dragging around with me to all the boring tourist sights—"

"Oh no, that would be awesome!" said Jasmine. "I'd love to visit some of those places again. I haven't been to most of them since I was a kid. It'll be cool to go back and, like, see how they've changed. And you haven't been to Orlando yet, right? I never turn down a chance to visit Disneyworld again," she said, chuckling. "Just tell me when and I'll come pick you up in my car. How about tomorrow? Or the day after? I've got a couple of days off from my job at the marina and we could do a whole bunch of stuff together."

Ellie looked helplessly at the other girl. "Er… wouldn't you rather spend your days off with Blake?"

"Huh? Why would I wanna spend them with *him*?" Jasmine looked astonished.

"Well, because he's… he's your boyfriend," said Ellie through gritted teeth.

"*My boyfriend?*" Jasmine gave a squeal of laughter. "You gotta be kidding me! Why would you think that Blake's my boyfriend?"

"Because I saw… I mean…" Ellie stammered. "I thought the two of you were together?"

"Blake's a cool guy and I like him a lot, but I wouldn't *date* him!" said Jasmine, wrinkling her nose. "He's *old!* He's, like, thirty-two or something."

"But... but the two of you seem so close. I mean..." Ellie hesitated, not wanting to admit that she had been spying on them two nights ago. "You... erm... you stay over at Blake's condo, don't you?"

"Oh, I was only there the night before last, but that was only 'cos Dad wanted Blake to keep an eye on me."

"What d'you mean? Why would he need to keep an eye on you?" asked Ellie, thoroughly confused now.

Jasmine glanced around, then lowered her voice and said: "I didn't wanna tell anyone but... well, Dad's told the police now, so I guess it'll all come out eventually." She took a deep breath. "I was at this party on the night that Walter Saunders got poisoned. It was at the marina, on one of the big superyachts owned by some rich dude. I kinda know someone who knows someone who knows the son of the rich dude... Anyway, we scored invitations—

me and Ava. It's like getting into a club, you know?" Jasmine winked at Ellie. "If you're a girl and you're young and pretty, it's easier to get past the bouncers. Anyway, Ava had to work her shift at *Hammerheads* first and I didn't wanna sit around waiting for her, so I went alone first."

Jasmine paused and looked a bit sheepish as she continued, "They were doing, like, all kinds of freaky stuff at the party. You know, like stimulant-enhanced cocktails and other stuff. I... I guess it was a bit dumb of me but I didn't want to look uncool so I joined in. I don't know what was in those drinks, but after a while I started feeling really weird. Like spaced out and wanting to puke and not being able to control my legs and stuff. I got scared, so I called Dad. He rushed over to the marina to pick me up—"

"That's why he left his shift so suddenly!" said Ellie.

"Right. He came and got me, and he wanted to take me to the hospital to get me checked out, but I was like: 'No way!' See, I've got this college scholarship, and if they find out that I was at that kind of party, with all the booze and drugs... I could lose the whole scholarship!"

"And that's why your father wouldn't explain his movements that night either," said Ellie, beginning to understand everything at last.

"Yeah. It was all my fault, really," said Jasmine ruefully. "I was, like, really freaking out and getting hysterical. In the end, Dad agreed not to take me to the hospital, but he said I had to come back here to the resort, so Blake could check me over instead. Dad's really good friends with Blake," Jasmine explained. "They started working at Sunset Palms at the same time and hit it off instantly. The two of them go fishing together and meet up for drinks sometimes, so I've seen a lot of Blake. He's always telling me stuff, like I shouldn't drink booze on an empty stomach, and I have to be careful with fad diets…" Jasmine rolled her eyes again, then said grudgingly, "But I guess he's just trying to look after me. He's kinda like the big brother I never had."

Ellie stared at the other girl, horrified at how she had gotten everything wrong.

"Anyway, Blake said I should be fine but, just in case, someone had to stay with me and watch me for, like, twenty-four hours or something," Jasmine continued. "So I went home with Dad, but the next day, when Dad got taken in for questioning and he thought he might have to remain in custody, he got super worried about me spending the night alone. I was like: 'I'm totally fine!' But he wouldn't believe me. So in the end, I agreed to sleep over at Blake's condo, just to make Dad happy. But it was really dumb, you know, 'cos I went out that night anyway. Blake couldn't stop me. I mean, it's not like I'm ten years old, right?" Jasmine grumbled. "It was no big deal anyway. I went to hang out with some friends in downtown St. Pete and I was back by midnight. I told Blake not to wait up for me—it's not my fault if he didn't listen." Jasmine looked at Ellie curiously. "How did you know that I was staying over at Blake's place?"

"Oh… erm… it must have been something you said before," mumbled Ellie. She felt like a fool. She also felt awful for how she'd treated Blake and what she'd said to him.

"Well, Jasmine and I had better get going," said Sol, interrupting Ellie's thoughts as he rose from Aunt Olive's lounge chair.

"Oh, you're welcome to join us," said Aunt Olive, indicating an empty cabana beside them.

Sol chortled. "Can you imagine Mr. Anderson's face if he saw me out here in a cabana with the guests? He would probably already have a fit if he'd seen me sitting and talking with you just now."

"Well, I would tell him that you're *my* guest," Aunt Olive declared.

Sol smiled. "Thanks for the invite, but actually I can't wait to get home. Be nice to take a shower in my own bathroom, make a cup of coffee in my own kitchen." He turned back to Ellie. "The reason I came out here was to find you, Ellie. I wanted to say thank you, for finding the real killer and helping me prove my innocence."

"Oh, no... I didn't really... I mean, the police would have found out the truth eventually," said Ellie, embarrassed. "I didn't really do anything—"

"You believed in me," said Sol solemnly. "That means a lot."

Ellie flushed with pleasure. A few minutes later, as she watched father and daughter walk back to the main resort complex, she decided that she didn't regret getting involved in the case—even if it had meant nearly getting eaten by an alligator!

Chapter Thirty-Two

"I'm going to order another cocktail, dear. Would you like one too?" asked Aunt Olive, perusing the drinks menu tucked into the side of the cabana canopy. "How about trying a Jungle Bird? Or a Zombie? The Rum Runner sounds delicious too."

"Oh no, I'm sticking with a good ol' piña colada from now on," said Ellie.

"I thought you'd be a bit more adventurous with your cocktail choices after taking that class."

"It was all this dabbling in other cocktails that got me into trouble in the first place!" said Ellie. "Maybe if I'd never gone to Rob Saunders's cocktail workshop, I wouldn't have got involved in the whole case."

"Speaking of Rob, have you heard? Apparently he's opening a big, swanky cocktail bar in downtown St. Pete—the first of its kind in Tampa Bay! He was busily bragging about it in the lobby when I saw him earlier," said Aunt Olive.

"Really? So have they sorted out Walter Saunders's will?"

Aunt Olive nodded. "Norman told me that he was planning to have a private meeting with Rob and Tonya last night. It sounds like Rob got good news about his inheritance—enough to immediately go full speed ahead with his business plans!"

"What about Tonya?" asked Ellie. "Did you hear if she got her share too?"

"No, I haven't seen Norman today so I haven't heard how the meeting went."

Aunt Olive gave Ellie a sideways look, then said, "You know who else I haven't seen today? Blake. I thought he would have been around, looking for you, after hearing what had happened last night. He's normally so quick to show concern for you and check that you're OK."

Ellie flushed and looked down. "Erm... Blake and I are sort of... not talking to each other at the moment," she said.

"What do you mean, 'not talking to each other'?" asked Aunt Olive. "I've never heard of such nonsense! You sound like children in a playground. Are you telling me that the two of you still haven't kissed and made up?"

"Uh... no..."

"Why ever not?"

Ellie squirmed. "It's... it's my fault, really. There was a terrible misunderstanding and I... I jumped to conclusions."

"Well, just go and tell him, then."

"I can't!" cried Ellie.

Aunt Olive looked astonished. "Why not?"

"Because... because it's just too humiliating!" said Ellie miserably. "I'd have to tell Blake what a huge idiot I've been and... and... apologize and... I can't face him."

Aunt Olive made a tutting noise. "You know what they say about pride not keeping you warm at night."

"It's not just that," said Ellie quickly. She sighed. "I was thinking, this is probably all for the best. I mean, it's already December. Christmas is just around the corner, and after that I'll be returning to England in the new year. So this relationship was never going to go anywhere."

"So? Just enjoy it as a vacation fling," said Aunt Olive, waving a hand.

"But it's never that simple. There are feelings involved. People get hurt," Ellie protested.

"All right, so if it does turn into something that's more than a fling—so what? How do you know that it would 'never go anywhere,' as you say?"

"Because we'd be living on opposite sides of the Atlantic!" said Ellie. "You know what they say: most long-distance relationships fail. Besides, how would we even do it? Do we talk every day? Do we try to visit each other every few months? And what about later on? Would I have to move to America? Would Blake be willing to live in England? There are just so many obstacles and complications…"

Aunt Olive shook her head in exasperation. "Really, poppet! You're beginning to sound like your sister Karen! You can't always predict what's going to happen in life. Sometimes you just have to get in the boat and see where the river takes you. Besides, when it comes to love, I think you need to grab any chance for happiness with both hands. It's not that easy to find someone special, you know. Trust me, I've dated more men than you've had hot dinners." She reached out and patted Ellie's hand. "Anyway, this is all jumping ahead of yourself. Why don't you just open your heart to the possibilities and see what happens?"

Ellie didn't answer. Instead, she sighed again and looked out at the waves rolling onto the beach. Aunt Olive was silent too for a few moments, then suddenly she stood up and said:

"You know what we need? A walk on the beach."

Ellie looked at her quizzically. "Now?"

"Yes, now," said her aunt, grabbing her elbow and hauling her to her feet.

"But I thought you were going to order another cocktail," said Ellie.

"I've changed my mind," said Aunt Olive briskly. "Come along. The sun is just on the horizon and it's the perfect time for a stroll along the shore. You haven't collected any seashells yet, have you? They would be the perfect souvenir of your trip! You know this is one of the best places in Central Florida to find specimens of conches and whelks... and don't forget sand dollars! You can't go home without picking up one of those!"

Ellie was puzzled by her aunt's sudden enthusiasm for mollusks, but she obediently kicked off her flip-flops and padded barefoot across the soft white sand after the older woman. Aunt Olive hustled her toward the empty expanse of beach near the waterline, but Ellie had barely bent over to start hunting for shells when her aunt said:

"Oh, blast—I've forgotten my glasses. You stay here, poppet. I'll just pop back to our cabana to get them."

Ellie nodded, not even raising her head. She had just spotted a chunky cone-shaped shell sticking out of the sand in front of her right toe and she bent to pick it up. It was a beautiful glossy caramel color, with several whorls and a pointed spire at one end.

I wonder what this is… a conch? Ellie thought. She tucked it into the palm of her left hand and continued walking, her eyes glued to the sand in front of her. Soon she paused to pick up another shell, this time in a flat fan-shape, with beautiful reddish-brown markings across its mottled surface—almost in the form of tiny zigzags. It reminded her of the scallop shells she'd seen in restaurants, used as fancy dishes to serve food on, and she wondered if this was some kind of scallop as well.

She tucked it with the first shell she'd found and continued walking. She soon found herself engrossed in the hunt. There was something wonderful and soothing about forgetting everything and just living in that moment: scanning the beach for shells, enjoying the golden light of the fading sun, feeling the sea breeze soft against her skin…

Ellie walked across a long expanse of beach littered with several fragments of shells but saw nothing else worth picking up. She was now quite a long way down the beach and she was just wondering if she should turn back when she saw something half-buried in the sand, just at the edge of the waves. She waded into the water, relishing the feel of the cold foam around her ankles and the wet sand between her toes. She bent to scoop up the round white object and held it up, turning it over and looking at it curiously.

The pure white surface of the shell looked ethereal in the fading light. It wasn't a perfect circle—more of a flat, round blob—and it had notches around the edge. But the most fascinating thing of all was the faint imprint in the center, which looked like a five-petaled flower. Ellie had never seen anything so delicate and beautiful. It also seemed incredibly fragile. She was just wondering how to carry it safely back when she heard her aunt coming up behind her.

"Aunt Olive—look what I found! Do you know what this shell is? It's absolutely gorgeous!"

"That's a sand dollar."

Ellie gasped at the sound of the deep male voice and whirled around. Blake was standing a few feet behind her. The breeze ruffled his sun-streaked brown hair and the fading light played across the handsome features of his face.

"Hi Ellie."

Ellie swallowed. Her head was a tumult of thoughts and emotions, and her tongue felt as if it had stuck to the roof of her mouth. What was Blake doing here?

As if reading her mind, Blake gave her a wry smile and said: "Your aunt came to find me and… uh… insisted that I should come walk down this stretch of the beach."

I might have known—Aunt Olive is meddling and trying to play Cupid! thought Ellie, mentally rolling her eyes.

"I… I thought you were in Orlando," she said, finding her voice at last.

"I was, last night. I had a medical conference there. But I got back late this morning." He hesitated. "I had a backlog of stuff to do at the clinic and I didn't hear about what happened at the gator farm until a couple of hours ago. I was going to come and find you, but then I was called to an emergency in one of the guest suites. Tonya Saunders had assaulted the estate lawyer and scratched his face badly."

"*What?*" Ellie gasped, her own problems temporarily forgotten.

"Yeah, apparently she wasn't happy with the reading of the will," said Blake with an ironic look. "It seems that Walter Saunders had hired a private investigator to tail his wife for a few months. He knew about her affair with the yacht captain, among others, and he'd rewritten his will to cut her out of everything. She's been left without a cent, other than the clothes and jewelry he gave her. It turns out even the yacht he 'bought' her isn't actually in her name."

Ellie shook her head and gave a small smile. "So there *is* karma after all…"

There was an awkward silence, then Blake cleared his throat and said, pointing to the white object in her hands, "Sand dollars aren't actually shells, you know—they're related to sea urchins and starfish. When they're alive, they're covered in fuzzy spines and they look purplish gray. But when they die, the sun bleaches their exoskeletons white. That's what you're holding."

"Why are they called sand dollars?" asked Ellie.

"People thought they looked like the old Spanish silver dollar coins, that's why. But there's also a legend which says they're coins lost by mermaids or used by the people of Atlantis before it sank into the ocean."

"Oh. Right." Ellie couldn't help thinking that it seemed absurd they should be standing there, talking about shells, when there were so many other things that needed to be said. There was so much she wanted to say to Blake, but it felt as if the words were jammed in her throat. Somehow, keeping the conversation on a neutral topic felt easier and at least got them talking.

She looked down, fumbling with the other shells she'd found. "Erm... do you know what this one is?" She held up the caramel-colored spiral shell.

"That's a Florida fighting conch shell. They're one of the most common shells found on the beaches here." Blake came a bit closer to look at the shells in her palm. "And the other one looks like a zigzag scallop."

"Oh, I was right! It *is* a scallop," said Ellie, pleased. Then she thought: *I can't keep avoiding the subject. I owe Blake an apology and I have to clear things up between us.*

Taking a deep breath, Ellie raised her head to meet his eyes and said: "Blake... I'm sorry. It... it was a terrible misunderstanding. I didn't know about your friendship with Sol and how close you are to Jasmine. She told me why she was staying over at your place that night... I shouldn't have jumped down your throat like that. I should have trusted you—"

"No, it's my fault too," said Blake. "I should have just told you everything the night I called to cancel our date. It's just that Jasmine was hysterical that night and Sol was so worried and they both made me promise not tell anyone about what had happened—"

"No, no, you were right. You had to keep doctor's confidentiality. I shouldn't have expected… You see, I had a terrible experience with my ex-boyfriend. He… he cheated on me," said Ellie in a tight voice. "And when I saw you and Jasmine coming out of your condo door, it seemed like some kind of awful déjà vu. I suppose I lost all sense of perspective. But… but I'm not really like that," she added. She gave him a weak smile, attempting to make a joke. "I'm not some crazy, jealous madwoman, honest! I just… I suppose I overreacted because I—" She stopped.

"Yes?"

Ellie felt her cheeks flushing hot. "Well, I… I've really developed feelings for you."

Something flashed in Blake's brown eyes and a slow smile spread across his face. He came even closer, so that Ellie could feel the warmth of his body. They were standing together now in the shallows, the waves rolling past their bare feet and the cold water swirling around their toes. The last rays from the setting sun bathed them in a soft orange glow.

Ellie looked up into Blake's eyes, feeling her heart thumping wildly in her chest. She held her breath, her body rigid with anticipation, as Blake leaned slowly forward. He was so close… his lips hovering inches from hers…

"Blake! *Blake!*"

Blake jerked back and they turned to look at the figure striding across the beach toward them. At first, Ellie thought that it was Aunt Olive, then she realized that it was a younger woman. She was tall and attractive, with a curvaceous figure and straight blonde hair that blew back from her face in a sleek curtain.

She came up to them, beaming and panting slightly, and said breathlessly:

"Blake! Honey, I've been searching all over the resort for you!"

She threw her arms around his neck and engulfed him in a hug. Blake reeled back slightly as she reached up to give him a peck on the cheek. Then the woman let go and spun around to face Ellie.

"Hi there!"

"Erm… hello," Ellie stammered. She felt overwhelmed by everything that was happening: first Blake had been about to kiss her, and now this woman…!

Blake cleared his throat and said: "Ellie, this is Gina… my… my ex-girlfriend."

The woman held her hand out to Ellie, who took it in a daze. "Nice to meet you, Ellie. You staying at the resort?"

Ellie nodded dumbly.

"It's a great place, huh? When I heard that Blake had gotten himself a job here,

I had to come and check it out—especially when I knew I could get a free stay," she added with a coy look at Blake.

He started to say something, but Gina cut him off:

"Honey, what are you doing out here on the beach? It's Happy Hour!" She gave Blake a playful slap on the arm. "Guess what? I've reserved a cabana for us and I've ordered your favorite cocktail. The Old Fashioned, right? See, I still remember! Come on, it's probably been delivered already and it's waiting for you..."

She turned to Ellie with a smile. "Wanna join us?"

THE END

About The Author

USA Today bestselling author H.Y. Hanna writes fun cozy mysteries filled with clever puzzles, lots of humor, quirky characters - and cats with big personalities! She is known for bringing wonderful settings to life, whether it's the historic city of Oxford, the beautiful English Cotswolds or the sunny beaches of coastal Florida.

After graduating from Oxford University, Hsin-Yi tried her hand at a variety of jobs, including advertising, modelling, teaching English, dog training and marketing... before returning to her first love: writing. She worked as a freelance writer for several years and has won awards for her novels, poetry, short stories and journalism.

A globe-trotter all her life, Hsin-Yi has

lived in a variety of cultures, from Dubai to Auckland, London to New Jersey, but is now happily settled in Perth, Western Australia, with her husband and a rescue kitty named Muesli. You can learn more about her and her books at: www.hyhanna.com.

Join her Readers' Club Newsletter to get updates on new releases, exclusive giveaways and other book news!

https://www.hyhanna.com/newsletter

Acknowledgments

As ever, I must thank my beta readers, Kathleen Costa and Connie Leap, for their help with the manuscript and in particular, making sure American characters speak and act authentically! And I'm always grateful to the rest of my publishing team for being so flexible and doing everything they can to ensure a smooth release schedule.

Last but not least, I can never thank my wonderful husband enough for his support, help and encouragement.

www.ingramcontent.com/pod-product-compliance
Lightning Source LLC
Chambersburg PA
CBHW030952190726
48285CB00004BB/1306